Praise for Jennifer Anne Gordon

"Dark, twisted, and lyrical. This book destroyed me, and I couldn't put it down." –

- **Kassie Romo of Reedsy**

"An exhilarating story packed with magnificently complex characters, psychological intrigue, and horror..."

- **Prairies Book Review**

"Beautiful, Frightening, and Silent by Jennifer Anne Gordon will squeeze your heart, take your breath, and keep you turning pages."

- **Readers Favorite 5 Star Review**

"Gordon's lyrical words flow invoking vivid imagery that comes alive making you feel and taste them. This is a haunting tale of love, hate and fate with characters that are both broken and beautiful, and that you may both love and hate. Gordon's use of time added a level of suspense that kept me on the edge of my seat determining who and what was real and alive. The twist at the end made me wonder if we will get more to this story. I highly recommend this beautifully written haunting tale!"
- **Book Review Crew (Authors on the Air Network)**

"Harrowing, heartbreaking, emotional, romantic and fantastical. If you have ever lost someone or regretted something in your life that cannot be fixed, you will feel this story in your gut."
- **David Pratt, Author**

ISBN-978-1-7354021-0-9 (ebook)

ISBN-978-1-7354021-1-6 (paperback)

Cover design by: Don Noble (Rooster Republic Press)

Library of Congress Control Number: 2018675309

Printed in the United States of America

From Daylight to Madness

The Hotel #1

Jennifer Anne Gordon

Livre Maison {book house}

Part I

Willows whiten, aspens quiver,
Little breezes dusk and shiver
Through the wave that runs for ever
By the island in the river
Flowing down to Camelot.
Four grey walls, and four grey towers,
Overlook a space of flowers,
And the silent isle imbowers
The Lady of Shalott.

-    Lord Alfred Tennyson

Prologue

April 1873

He cried for about three minutes, his little voice sounded powerful at first, fighting, and strong. His cries found their way to her ears, which had always been so desperate for love. His strange sounds immediately sounded like home, and like love, but those sounds very quickly changed. Of course, it all happened so fast, she did not even know it was a 'him' at this point. It was just crying, just screaming.

Just *home*.

There was an almost immediate feeling of removal, followed by a rush of emotion, pain, and even more blood. So much so, that the expulsion of this texture felt as though she were still giving birth. She did not even realize her part in all of this was done. She had done 'what she could' and the rest was up to God.

He made guttural sounds, uneven, jagged bursts. Gasping sounds that seemed to grow muffled, as if there were a thick viscous liquid poured down his throat. It was a drowning of sorts; the irony was that he was drowning outside of her. He was drowning on this crisp spring night in the slightly dusty and salt-tinged air of Portland Maine.

It was painful to her, those begging breaths that seemed to reach out and grasp. The pain was not real, not in a physical sense, not anymore. But the emotional pain, she was beginning to feel it now. In the seemingly endless minutes that passed, she had already come to know his sounds. Those frenzied sounds, the way they stampeded into her, she knew she would feel this forever. They were carved into her like initials on the old Oak tree in the small yard of the poorhouse where she grew up. She knew that the echo of these cries would last years. Their scars would grow pale over time but would always be there, marking her memory; these little auditory footprints that would feel like kicks insides of her.

The part of her that made him, that held him inside her body, was scarred now. Ruined.

There was pain for months before this. It went unsaid. It was 'to be expected.' At her age, there should have always been 'some discomfort.' She mentioned it, or at least she thought she must have when she would visit her physician. His office was an uncomfortable and dusty room located in the back of the Apothecary.

During her visits, she would describe what she was feeling inside of her. She said it was like butterflies at first, the kicking, the movement . . . but over time it dwindled. The butterflies became moths, and eventually they were just dust in a jar, on a shelf, inside of her body.

She is not quite as sure now, she is trying to remember, and maybe she never mentioned it at all, or at least not enough. She should have made it clearer, made her voice heard; the feeling that something inside her took a wrong turn, that it somehow went wrong. She should have said that the excited feeling she had deep below her belly, was still there, but it felt slower; did she say that? And if she said it, did they hear her; was she heard?

Did they care? Worse, did *she* care?

She thought she would not be able to take the sound anymore, the plaintive and desperate cries from this small creature that lived inside her, it was too much. Could none of them do anything to make it stop? She tried to push herself out of the bed. She tried in vain to reach for something that was not there, that was never there.

Love.

She imagined the hands, the small fingers almost like cats' claws. She wanted to feel the sharp nasty cuts from this kitten of hers. This little thing filled with so much fear, anger, and love, that in its excitement it hurt her. It reached out and scratched. It bit.

She bled.

But as she sat up, the room swam around her and the darkness crept in front the corners. It almost overtook her, which was when she noticed it; the sudden silence. She let herself fall back onto the bed as the early morning light turned from daylight to madness, and then of course, there was nothing, there was nothing at all.

Her hair which had been soaked with sweat, now hung cool and damp against her face. The blood soaking the sheets, which were warm only moments ago, began to thicken in the cool air and feel stiff against her skin.

Isabelle thought it would all be different, she imagined throughout these not quite nine months, that the room would be warm, that someone would have thought to light candles. She always pictured a healing fire in the fireplace in the corner of the largest room, in their small house. She could imagine Henry's face, it would be warm, appreciative, it would seem almost, if not quite exactly, to look like love. This expression of his, it would live in the house next to where love would be, if it had only ever moved in, adjacent to it, holding its hand, living with it. A feeling next to love.

He would hand her the baby and Henry would say, "Here he is, our boy, our Oscar."

It was not nine months. No, of course, it was not. It was seven, maybe seven and a half – she should know. She should have always known, the exactness of it, the moment of conception. The moment that she would be more than just a 'her,' the moment she would be a mother, the thing she was always expected to be, and until now, and *even now* . . . was not.

She did not know; she did not know any of this. She was a mother, who now was not. What is that called? Is there a name for that; the silent grief, the mourning that is best ignored, tidied away, lest it make someone uncomfortable?

There was blood on the floor, it was mixed with tissue, there were pieces of her, and pieces of Oscar. She thought perhaps his little hands had held onto something inside of her and pulled it out on his way. As if he knew, it was not his time to leave.

She closed her eyes, and a cry filled the air.

His cries, Oscar's cries, not hers; Isabelle had not cried.

Not yet.

There would be an inexpensive grave that simply read, 'Baby Boy,' when it should have said his name; a name that her husband would want to save for 'the next one.' As if *this* one was not real. As if a life existing in three small minutes somehow meant less than a life lived in thirty years.

This thing that happened, she could almost hear the neighbors whispering about it, their voices thick with judgement and colored on the ends with fear. Whispering about the birth that did not happen, the baby that did not live.

The life that never happened – except it did.

There was Oscar; he was there, for three minutes. There were no loving looks, no warmth of candles and dim soothing firelight. There was pain. There was blood. There was relief.

6

There was three minutes of crying.

There was Oscar.

Then, then, there was nothing.

Chapter 1

She could of course hear so much more than they had wanted her to, in the moments after it all happened . . .

She could hear Henry's mother, who only four minutes before the 'nothing,' had held Isabelle's hand, and had been with her. Now of course, in the one minute since 'the nothing' Isabelle could hear her angry whispers. The blaming words, referring to something Isabelle must have done wrong, to make him born like this. The little cord wrapped around his neck, not stopping all his air, but stopping most of it.

Even if he had lived, she understood that there would have always been whispers, "he would have been wrong." There was a pause; a silence that felt to Isabelle's ear's like concrete slowly being poured. It was taking up the space that even Henry was not awful enough to fill with his inane words. He was always a man with a lack of emotional understanding. It was as if he would never be able to comprehend love or grief. She could hear their whispers, Henry, and his Mother, "It is better he be dead than having the burden placed on you."

Silence.

The pause stretched out in all directions, and finally made its way back to her and carved another piece of her away when it did.

9

The nothing.

The three minutes of fighting cries from a baby too small to have a chance, Isabelle, from her bed tried to mouth the words "I should hold him."

The door closed and she was left there, in the room, with 'the nothing.' Unsure if she had said anything or not. She pushed herself up once again from the bed. She looked to the corner of the room to the top drawer of their finest bureau. They had pulled it out and filled it with blankets that they had warmed downstairs by the stove. That little space would have been his bed for tonight, for the little guest that arrived too soon. As she stretched up, she thought she could see inside, but all there was, was blood.

And nothing.

Isabelle was able to move herself towards the end of the bed, leaving the red wake of blood on the sheets behind her. The blood immediately chilled the sheets, and left her nightgown soaked and heavy. She looked down and it seemed to be an almost black color, and she felt as if she were sitting in a bog.

The room around her pulsed with silence, and the edges of her vision danced in and out of darkness. She was out of breath, there seemed to be stones placed inside of her body pulling her back down. Her head collapsed on the bed, she could feel the blood dampen her hair, and leave a mark against her cheek like a kiss. She was able to place her bare feet on the ice-cold floor. It chilled her with an ache that reached up towards her knees and between her legs.

The door opened without warning, her mother in-law, who had always asked to be called Minnie instead of mother, stood in front of her. She blurred in and out of Isabelle's hazy focus.

"I would like to be able to hold Oscar," Isabelle whispered this, her voice dry and hoarse from hours of screaming during her labor. She did not lift her head up off the bed.

"No, no, that won't do anyone any good, here, drink this."
Minnie handed her a cup of warm brown liquid, with a deep red hue.
To call it tea would be a lie, though it was handed to her in one of their
finest teacups, white, with delicate blue flowers and just the hint of the
gold leaf that once sat proud against the edges. This cup had a small
chip on the rim near the place Isabelle placed her mouth.

The liquid was bitter, it tasted like a combination of licorice,
rotted leaves, and defeat. It went without saying that it was laudanum.

Before Isabelle could protest, or at least ask to be able to see
her son. Minnie was pulling her up off the bed, leading her roughly by
the arm to stand in the corner. Minnie stripped the sheets off the bed in
a perfunctory manner that was only broken up at times by grunts of
disgust.

Minnie, who did not know where in this house the laundry was
taken, balled up the soiled sheets and placed them in the corner. She
moved to Isabelle and unbuttoned the long white sleeping dress that
was soaked through with death. Minnie's fingers became slicked with
the cold blood, making the buttons challenging for her already gnarled
fingers. The sleeping gown was dropped to the floor next to them, as if
balling that up and tossing it with the rest of the things would have
been too much added effort. It landed heavily on the floor near
Isabelle's feet. The bloodstains seemed to be growing out from around
her, like vines.

Blood continued to trail down Isabelle's legs as she stood
there. She leaned against the wall, making sure to keep most of her
body away from it, for fear of staining the pale green silk pattern of the
wallpaper. She shivered in the cool but not fresh air, and waited to be
told what would happen next.

"Don't just stand there; do you want to get even sicker? Put on
a fresh gown." Minnie called this over her shoulder with efficiency
and a stinging disappointment as she pulled a fresh nightdress from the
bureau and handed it without looking at Isabelle's now naked body.
She was unable to meet Isabelle's eyes.

11

Mother Minnie made the bed up with fresh sheets and was almost done by the time Isabelle had managed to pull a fresh gown over her head. Her arms were ungainly and slow. Her coordination hampered with the drink and the blood loss.

The loss, all of it, she should not diminish it by just thinking blood.

She was led back towards the bed and told to finish her tea. She did as she was told and almost immediately could not remember taking the last sip, just moments before the darkness at the edge of her sight finally took over. That darkness had been dancing there for countless minutes, until it finally waltzed her away. It brought her there to 'the nothing.'

As she faded away, she thought she could hear the ocean, a piano, and a baby crying.

It was the sound of the door closing that brought her back. Her eyes open. The room spins around her as she raises her head off the flattened pillow. She tries to sit up and move her legs apart, but she feels the dried blood pull at the skin on her upper thighs. They feel almost adhered to each other like glue. This feeling of resistance on her skin fills her with shame for some unknown reason. She closes her legs again quickly, and tries instead to move herself to a sitting position with just her arms.

She sees Henry. He is standing near the door. His head moves slowly as he surveys the room around him with a reverent observance. His eyes trace the shape of her body as she lies in the bed, but he does not register her as being anything more than a lumpy set of bed linens that were fresh hours ago and are now filthy. His face travels through shock, to sadness, and finally lands on disgust.

He sees the blood-soaked sheets on the floor, mingled with her nightdress. He sees blood in small pools, some liquid; others are filled with tissue, the size of fists. The vibrant red had turned to a molasses colored black around the edges as these viscus reminders aged through the night. The visceral memories living longer than the three minutes of crying that will no longer be mentioned.

"This room needs to be cleaned up." He says this, as his eyes finally land on her face. The rest of the house outside of these dingy walls of this room are quiet, the doctor is gone, Mother Minnie as well. Henry, not a man to get on his hands and knees to clean a floor is the only one left, and of course her.

"It's not good for you, mentally to be in here with all of . . . with all of this." His hands gesture vaguely around the room. His eyes do not leave her face now, they don't make any more contact with the debris of their loss.

"I can get you something." His words are tentative, unsure. They sound like someone walking over a frozen pond at the beginning of spring. Each one could lead to a crack, at first, they splinter and then break in two.

"More tea?" Isabelle asks. She does not say Laudanum. This is done the same way that she knows she is now not supposed to say Oscar.

"Oh, actually I was thinking of a bucket with some rags for the mess. But yes, I can bring you more tea as well, for when you are done with the cleaning."

Yes, the cleaning of course.

"You will feel better I am sure, once this is taken care of." He stood there awkwardly for a few more moments; he shifted his weight from one foot to the other. It seemed almost as if he were about to walk across the room towards her, reach his hand out, place it gently against her cheek. This was only ever just an imagined, shared moment of comfort.

He did not do any of this. Instead, he ended up clearing his throat several times, looking down at his own feet, and finally, after a respectable amount of time had passed, he turned sharply and exited the room in an almost militaristic style.

He returned quickly, holding a bucket with not quite warm water, a bar of soap and several already stained rags. Isabelle could hear Henry's thoughts as he gathered the supplies, that it would be a waste to use good towels to clean this up. The good towels should be saved, used for when she is drying their finest of their cutlery and bowls.

He places everything just inside the door and closes it quickly behind him again, the disgust and fear were apparent in the speed in which she heard him retreating, getting as far from her, and this place as possible.

Would they ever be able to lay in the bed again, would the deep red stains ever fade, would they ever sink with the heaviness of stones and find their way so deep within the mattress that they no longer existed?

She did not think so.

She wrapped the rags around her hands, like gloves, and started first by picking up the larger pieces, the clots that looked like the angered fists of men who fight in public houses for fun. Without understanding quite what she was supposed to be doing with them, she walked slowly to that top drawer. It was still filled with blankets. This drawer still wears the costume and playing the role of the small bed for the little guest.

She placed the tissue fragments, the evidence of her unspoken crime against their marriage and would be family, into that top drawer. She closed it quietly, as if to let them all sleep.

Though she tried hard to be careful, she noticed that her hands, her fingers mostly, were covered in blood. Without thinking, she walked to their bed and pushed the mattress to the side a bit, and underneath the place she would eventually sleep tonight, she wrote his name in blood, in her blood.

In their blood.

Oscar

She thinks again of the little grave that will likely be nameless, just a sad place that she will someday ask to visit. She knows she will make the request often at first, and then perhaps it will be just once a month. Later in life when she is older and tired, and the pain of whatever this loss is finally fades, she will see his grave only on the anniversary of his birth.

His death.

His three minutes.

She wonders if it will be then that she finally cries, finally allows herself to feel this. Until then she knows that she will at least have this, this small remembrance of the boy who would have been, the boy that was.

Oscar.

Chapter 2

In the weeks that immediately followed, Henry, Mother Minnie, and the few others that came in and out of her room only spoke to her in whispers. She would respond in a normal voice, and they would always immediately shush her. She was told she should be taking it easy; she should be resting. As if talking at a normal volume would somehow exhaust her more than her grief would. They all behaved as if using her voice would somehow make the room swim around her more than the great loss of blood and life constantly now did.

Mother Minnie was there seemingly around the clock during the first week. She would come over and prepare meals that were somehow a combination of meats that were cooked so long they were tough like leather, and vegetables boiled to the point that they would dissolve in your mouth. The taste and texture would remind Isabelle of playing "cook" a couple times when she was small. She would pull grass from the front yard of the almshouse, gathering as many small handfuls as she could at a time without it becoming too noticeable. She would place them in boiling water and would stir it until it was thick and swampy. She would beg the other children, including her friend Molly, to taste it. She could tell by their sour grimaces that they had hated the way it looked and tasted. Yet, Isabelle always took pride in the fact that she made something, something that was hers.

After that initial first week, the whispering continued but Minnie's meals were no longer something to be counted on or expected. Though Isabelle was still dizzy every time she moved her head, and her heart still beat ceaselessly against the rocks inside of her if she would walk more than just a few feet, she knew that once again the 'duties of the house' were hers and hers alone. She was silently given back her role again, as wife, maid, cook, and soon she assumed, would once again be the plaintive, patient, and now silent, lover.

That last part would mean that Henry would have to begin once again, to look directly at her. Currently he would whisper in her direction, but he had yet to look in her eyes, which were tinged red around the edges. This was not from tears, because of course there had been none, but instead it was from the tea she sipped slowly throughout the day. The earthy taste coating her mouth, made her grow more and more bitter with each passing whisper-filled day.

She was at the sink, using their unstained towels to dry the teacups that she would leave scattered throughout their small house like a trail through the woods, the breadcrumbs of her morning, and of her mourning. She would drink her tea throughout the day. She knew her schedule not by looking at the clock, or even by noticing the subtle changing white light creeping through the windows as it slowly burnished its way into the afternoon. Instead she had an understanding that when she would reach into the china cabinet and see only one teacup remaining, that the time had come to ready the house for Henry's return from work.

She would first gather the cups. She would let them soak in warm water. Then, she would try to make herself presentable by running her fingers through her long, almost unruly brown curls. She would pinch at her cheeks, the way she did when they were both young and still courting. That was when she wanted to seem fresh faced and comely. It was hard for her to remember what it was like to feel an eagerness to be loved, to be satisfied with that. Now, she does this same thing to stave off the paleness, the creeping dread, that death had kissed at her insides and left her rotting. Her once healthy skin was left feeling clammy and had a gray tinge to it.

18

She wonders if he can smell that on her, in the cold damp sweat that covers her body like lace. The delicate nature of rot, like a beautiful poisonous mushroom, the smell of a dead child's cries, and the bitterness of the medicinal tea seeping out of her like a demon's sulfuric calling card.

No.

She shakes her head; she clears her thoughts. She becomes again for a whisper of time, the woman she always hoped to be. The woman she was before this, the one became out of sad complacency. The woman he made her into; Henry found her and carved her from a simple stone wall, into sculpture. She is real now, because of him.

Where once there was only an idea of a person, now she was one, a wife, a mother . . . no, not that.

She always thought, as a child, she would be real, because of . . . her. Now she exists because of this tragedy, she is the dark lady; she is the sad witch in a house on a hill.

She would assume her position at the kitchen sink, looking out the small window that faced the street. She could see him coming, and it was then, that she would spring into action. She would wash the cups; she would dry them. She would place them neatly side by side like the gravestones of soldiers. She would use their best towels. She would be thankful that Henry had given her nothing but dirty rags to clean up that day.

So thankful.

So, so very thankful.

It would have been a shame to ruin these beautiful towels.

These are for the cups.

This was her job, to be thankful, to wash the dishes, to have pink lively cheeks. To turn towards him as he entered the room, her eyes bright, and mind brimming with ideas from the Woman's

19

Magazine that Henry allowed her to read, the one that taught her 'how to keep a house,' and how best to be a 'grateful and attractive' wife.

She was not doing her job these days. She saw him on the road and knew he was coming in, but still somehow, she failed to hear the door opening and closing. She failed to hear his heavy and deliberate steps as he entered the room behind her. He eventually made a mumbling sound as he tossed the daily newspaper onto the small table in the corner. She wondered if the words he said were meant for her, or were they were just noises, he made for himself. Did he do this, to fill the air and distance between them, or were they just meaningless sounds to take the place of words?

She did turn to him then, but where there were once her bright eyes, there was now only dullness staring into dullness. Her eyes had been overtaken with a slightly weepy almost seeping look. Her eyes for weeks were dazed and unfocussed. It was almost as if she was hearing and seeing things ten seconds after they happened. Her world was like this now; it existed in the past. It was a small but distinct divide in their worlds, it was just enough to leave both Isabelle and Henry utterly alone.

Together.

"I almost didn't think you were here. The house is quiet, and it hardly smells like there is dinner . . . Isabelle? Isabelle do you hear me?" Henry says all of this, and even though the words seem to take longer to travel to Isabelle's ears and then to her brain, she does eventually hear them. She most especially hears the concern in his voice, the concern that seemed to be at its strongest when he mentioned the word 'dinner.'

She turns to him; her movements are slow as if she fought against water and time; it takes what seems like months finally to face him. Months, and of course, the additional ten seconds she lives her life in that, is different to his.

She looks at him. They make eye contact and immediately his eyes lower as if he has suddenly become entranced by his own shuffling feet. His shoes were still caked with flour from the bakery and mud from the road while he travelled home. His feet seem overburdened and sad.

"I'm sorry, what was that? What was it you said?" Her voice lower in pitch and tone than it used to be, the words form slower and slower in her mouth, she creates them with more care, trying to make each one come out clearly, and without tragedy. It was as if each slurred word would remind them both that part of her strangles and destroys everything she had ever hoped to create, whether that be words, or a child.

So, she tried hard, to create the words, to make them live.

She blinked slowly and imagined the little cord wrapped around . . .

NO.

She never saw that. It is a memory that lives in her imagination alone. No, 'live' is the wrong word. She never saw his face, it does not live there, HE does not live there, and HE does not live anywhere . . .

"ISABELLE . . . the dinner?" Henry's voice was high-pitched and whinnied like a prancing pony.

She looked down at her hands, which were holding their finest and cleanest towel. She saw herself work it against the teacup, making it shine. This teacup spent its day holding poison and relief. She wiped at it until it was clean, until it looked the as it did when it was new. The when Isabelle was a new bride and Mother Minnie brought all these cups and plates over to them. As if the dishes would ensure their happiness.

The finest of gifts that no one ever asked for or wanted.

She should be thankful.

She placed the cup down in the line they were beginning to form between the breadbox and the sink. It did not fall quite in line with the rest of its friends, the rest of little white graves with pale blue flowers. Now that her hands were free, she reached up and pinched her cheeks, quickly bit at her lips. She remembered being told once that she was at her most beautiful when her lips were swollen, and her face flushed.

No one understood that she had this 'wanting' and comely appearance because she was stung by a minimum of nine wasps after accidentally allowing the kitchen door to slam shut. The wasps had easily angered and afterwards she was swollen and skittering on the inside. On the outside, she appeared quite different. This was the day when Henry had finally taken notice of her, all those years ago.

"Isabelle?"

The aching ten seconds that separates them exists now, in this pause, the room is filled with it. It presses against the walls and they are pushed further and further away, until the walls are hardly there at all. Their seeming absence makes her feel exposed and almost frightened . . .

"ISABELLE?"

"Yes?" She lowered her head and bit again at her lips in a more feverish attempt to look livelier, less ghoulish and frightening.

"Is there no dinner?" Henry seemed utterly perplexed at this, as if the thought had never once occurred to him that there might not be. Henry is a man who went from a mother's house, to a wife's house, with little interruption in his nightly schedule of when exactly it is that he wanted to eat his nightly meal. It has always worked the same way.

A Newspaper placed on the corner table, a few minutes of nice chitchat, "Mother how was your day?" Turned into, "Isabelle, how was your day?"

He never really listened to the answer. He kissed whichever one of them it was on the cheek, with his dry papery lips. He sat at a table . . . then dinner. It was always the same, different house, different woman, same routine.

"What have you been doing all day?" He asked this, suddenly whispering again at her. It was as though this was something he had forgotten to do before. He was distracted with the mention of food.

"I've been . . . busy, busy all day, I've been cleaning," she breathed in and looked around at the dusty clutter around them. "And I did some reading." She reaches up again to pinch at her cheeks, but she can feel them heating up and filling with color on their own.

Her cheeks are the strange pink hue, not of youth or love, but instead, of shame, the kind of reddish pink that happens in splotches over her skin during times of stress.

Henry sighs, and it sounds like he is giving up. It is a sigh of resignation. It came from deep inside of him. Birthed out of boredom and the exhaustion of working moderately hard at a job that was handed to him. He comes home hungry, not out of hard work but out of boredom.

Perhaps, that sigh is singed around the edges and burned ever so slightly with his own grief. To be fair, Isabelle would not know about that. He has never mentioned it and she cannot bring herself to ask.

"I think we need to talk, your behavior . . . no sorry, that is the wrong word. It is not your behavior, maybe it is your lack of . . . behaving." He cleared his throat and walked to the newspaper that had been casually discarded moments before. "Sorry, sorry, I am not good at this. When I spoke with Mother, she told me what to say, but you know I am not good with words, not the way she is." Henry stops. He looked up from the paper, and his eyes connected with Isabelle's.

He had a pleading almost mealy look to him. It is as if he wanted Isabelle to tell herself the insults and accusations, hurtful words that Henry may not have been man enough to say aloud.

He pulled out the chair, at their small breakfast table in the corner, the one that contained today's newspaper and a vase of rotting flowers. They were flowers that Isabelle could have sworn were fresh yesterday, or maybe that was the day before.

"You see, you just aren't bouncing back the way that we, I mean, I wanted. No, I am sorry, not wanted, hoped. You are not bouncing back the way we, I mean I, had hoped."

Isabelle lowered her head; she wanted to scream that her body has not quite even finished bleeding yet. That even though the blood has slowed down like a leaky faucet, that it still has not stopped, that the blood was a reminder that her grief was not just a feeling but also a smell. There was a weakness to it, to her. She thought that if the blood flowed between her legs than maybe she should not 'bounce back'. Maybe it was not time.

She was about to say these things, or at least something, when Henry continues.

"Also, you have not cried, and that's not normal. Mother said you should be crying. That would be healthy, and normal, more normal than this." He gestures towards the row of teacups in their graveyard, lined up like soldiers still wet from battle.

"I'm sorry; I know you believe I have done something wrong; I can see that." She stopped herself; she forms the words, so they are clear. "I am confused though . . ."

"Of course, you are, confusion is normal, you have had quite a shock. Also your medicines are probably making you . . ." His words fade away into almost a nothing of a sound, a hiss of air; his whispers grew quieter and quieter until they are dead.

"What I was trying to say, is that I was confused because I am not sure if you are upset with me because I am too sad, or if you are upset with me because I am not sad enough . . ." She felt herself age what to her was like a year just in her expression of these words.

Before she knows exactly what she has done, her arm sweeps through her line of soldiers, she does this with a rage and force she did not know was coming. Her hand connects with the freshest of the graves, the most recently cleaned and wiped teacup. Her little soldier falls to the floor and shatters in this battle. She makes a sound like a guttural wail. A frustrated yawp. This explosion of sound feels good inside her mouth and her throat. It feels like relief, and as she is about to express herself again, she hears it, a sound coming from Henry. It is that dreaded sound . . . the shush.

"Sssshhhhhhhhh . . . please, you need to be quiet. He does this in a harsh and scolding manner that lacks any comfort. He remains seated and still at the little breakfast table in the corner.

Isabelle hears her words swirling around in her head. When she hears them, they are awful, they sound like friendly fire in a war. The words sound like senseless deaths, the kind that happen when everyone is on the same side . . . she does not quite understand until she sees Henry's face that she was the one that fired the shot. She said the words out loud, and in an instant, she sees that her words killed the other imagined soldiers around her. The ones, if they existed at all, were in their way, trying to help, but in the confusion of grief, got lost in the smoke.

"Why can't I yell . . . will I wake the baby?" Her eyes filled with rage, but not with tears as she said this. She felt herself smile.

The echo of these words ricochets through their empty house. They bounce through the empty air, which is not filled with the aroma of a savory dinner being cooked. They hit Henry like a bullet. He is only grazed and left with a flesh wound; it is so different from the deep mortal wound that she has suffered. That one that has left her bleeding even still.

25

She hates herself. She hates him. She hates the three minutes of crying. Most of all she hates the nothing. She stares at the floor, the pieces of china that will be her duty to clean up, before or after she makes the dinner.

There is a silence; it is as strong as that stone wall that he created her out of. It was building itself up between them, and around her. The wall is made from anger, insults, missed meals, and dashed dreams. She feels that she is about to be closed in by each of these weighty stones. She hates to whisper but cannot help herself.

"I'm sorry."

"No, no need. You do not need to apologize. You are tired. That is all this is; you're tired." He gets up from the table, careful to sidestep the sharp pieces of shrapnel that litter the floor.

"I'm not sure that is what this is, this is more than that, I don't feel tired."

"Well, sometimes we are more tired than we think we are. It's probably extremely hard to think clearly when you are so tired." He chuckles a little as he whispers those words to her. There is a mean-spirited glee that sang and hissed underneath his words. The words felt like a threat when they finally reach her brain, ten long seconds after they hit her ears.

"Sandwiches will be fine; you can bring them into the study when you are finished with cleaning up that mess. You should take some tea up to the room and get some rest when you are done."

Isabelle looks out the little window above the sink, she has barely moved this entire time. She sees that the daylight has crept into night. She suddenly does feel that she might be tired, even more tired than she thinks she is.

Chapter 3

Isabelle spent the next several days on what she would describe as her best behavior. She rested. She cooked food that seemed to Henry's approval. It was both warm and tasteless, just the way he liked it. She continued with her tea but did attempt to bring some small sense of order and normalcy back into her life, she skipped the laudanum enhancer every third cup.

She would sit at the dining room table with Henry over meals, she would nod her head politely as they would both generally look towards each other's faces but never dared look directly into each other's eyes. They were like two almost lifelike dolls, being moved about in a child's gruesome game of an unhappy life.

She would ask questions about his day. She would ask about the bakery that had been in his family for generations. She asked the sort of silly and vapid questions a wife was expected to ask her husband after a day at work. "How many loaves of bread were made?" or "How hot was it in the kitchen today?" It was not until much later during the evenings when she had settled herself to bed, alone in their room that she would realize that though she asked questions, she did not remember hearing any answers.

She had the sneaking suspicion that they were not answered. That Henry was merely allowing her the small privilege of an imagined life, but he would not grace her with communication that ran on both directions.

Then again, there was probably a better chance that was just not listening. That the ten-second lapse between their lives had grown larger, so large that the ten seconds had become days, or months. She thought perhaps that days from now she would be staring out the kitchen window. She would be standing up on her tiptoes and imagining she could see over the rooftops of the buildings across the street. She would become lost in the idea that if she tried hard enough, she could see the ships coming and going in the port. When suddenly . . . she would hear his words from tonight's dinner, traveling through their great divide to finally reach her ears. "The kitchen was quite hot today, the humidity made it hard for the bread to rise."

She would turn her head expecting to see Henry, but her only company would be her shadow, a dark strange thing that had grown long and crooked in the afternoon light. She would reach her hand out towards nothing, her fingers stretching out and dipping through time. She would bring them back to her, and they would be covered in blood. She would remember the three minutes of crying, then she would take a sip of tea, and begin to forget them all again.

None of this was happening though, not now, not while she was resting. She was in bed. She was a good and thankful wife.

It was then that she sat up, startled. Though she had been laying in the bed for some time now, she had not quite finished undressing. Her feet were bare, yet she still wore layers of skirts and her corset, though loosened, still hung on her like an intoxicated embrace.

She strained her ears to hear the sounds underneath all the quiet. At first, she thought it was the batting of wings against the air, or the rustling papers. The ones that were so above her station she never bothered to understand. But, as she tiptoed towards her bedroom door, she could hear the sounds taking shape and becoming clearer, like a ship's sail cutting through fog.

28

It was whispering.

Trying not to make a sound, Isabelle crept towards the door and placed her hand around the doorknob. She turned it slowly, only to find it stopped after an inch. It had become unmoving in her hand. It was locked. Suddenly she felt as though the knob was growing hot against her skin. The whispering she heard downstairs were not whispers at all, but instead the sound of fire kissing the faded green silk of the wallpaper and curtains as it traveled towards her room. She took her hand away and backed up a few feet. She listened again and sniffed at the air for the undercurrent of smoke. There was nothing. She reached her hand out again and tenderly placed her fingers against the knob to find that it was cool.

She pressed her ear against the door but could not make out the words at all. All she could pick up on was the rhythm of the conversation. It seemed to canter like a horse, the quick back and forth of the sounds were deceitful in their rhythm. She was almost lulled by the musicality of it all. It was not until after several frantic minutes passed, that the conversation began to tire and slow, until it petered out to nothing.

She believed she could hear the front door open and then close at the foot of the stairs. The heavy footsteps grew louder like a rolling thunder as Henry came up to the second floor. She heard his pace lighten as he approached her room. Then almost delicately, she heard the key enter the lock, and with a few subtle clicks, she could hear the door unlock. Henry once again moved down the hall towards the guest room, where he had been spending his nights.

She opened the door hoping to startle him. She stepped into the hall behind him. She stood in the sootiest part of his shadow. He seemed unnaturally startled of her as he turned around, his eyes mixed fear and pity together seamlessly as if they were ingredients in a stew.

"Why are you out of bed, you should have been sleeping hours ago." He whispered at her, almost as if he were trying to coax a child back to sleep after waking from a nightmare.

29

"Who were you talking to? I heard voices." Isabelle asked.

"No, you couldn't have heard anything, there was no one here. Maybe you heard me as I was reading out loud; maybe that's what you heard." Henry's eyes once again seem only to be interested in his own feet as they shuffle against the wood floor. He was keeping time to music only he could hear.

"No, I heard something, so I got up, and my door was locked . . ." Isabelle was interrupted by Henry's derisive and dry half chuckle.

"Isabelle, listen to yourself, your door was not locked. You just opened it!"

"It was locked! I heard you talking to someone and then you came here and unlocked it. I know what happened!"

"You're imagining things . . . hearing things. You are tired. We know you're tired, you must have been dreaming, and then you woke up confused, that is all this is." Henry said, his head finally looking up, and his eyes travelling past her and into her room. His gaze traveled towards the now empty teacup next to her bed.

Isabelle stepped in front of Henry and blocked his view as she spoke. "You said we, before. Who is we?"

"I didn't say, 'we'"

"Yes, you did, you said 'we know you're tired.' Who is the other part of that we, you and who else?" Isabelle could hear the wonder in her voice as it tiptoed along a ledge, losing its balance and landing into paranoia.

"You sound shrill Isabelle, and you are getting yourself very worked up for no reason. Go back to your room and go to sleep."

"So, is it my room now? It used to be *our* room . . ."

"Isabelle, enough, please. You are tired, I am tired, let us not do this." Henry was already turning away from her; emotionally he was already in bed in the spare room, long asleep.

"Of course, you're tired. Sometimes we are more tired than we think we are." Isabelle could hear the anger burning at the edges of her voice. She imagined a fire starting, the one she heard before, hidden in the whispers behind the locked door.

She was once again alone in the hallway. Rather than turning back into her room, she stood there in the silence for a few minutes, waiting. When she was sure Henry would not come check on her, she tiptoed down the hall, and then down the stairs. She made sure to step gingerly on the fourth stair from the bottom, the one that would emit a loud creak like old bones, if you stepped on it with all your weight.

She is not sure what she is looking for, but she will know it when she sees it. She looked for the faint scar of someone else being in the house. She searched for the lingering residue of a lie told to her face. She can feel the lie in the air; its heaviness makes it hard to breath. Her eyes scan the front hallway and into the kitchen.

This is where she sees it, where she sees them. Like lovers pulling away from an embrace. Two teacups, one empty and the other still filled with, upon inspection a half-cup of lukewarm liquid. She knows that neither of them is hers. She closes her eyes and the memory of those whispers and lies burn inside her like a sickness. It leaves her standing here, weakened.

Chapter 4

She thought with certainty that she would not sleep that night. Yet, somewhere in the late hours of rage and distrust, she drifted off to a deep dreamless state. It was not quite sleep and more just an absence of awake. She did not rise in the morning feeling rested; she was just stiff, from several hours of not moving. The absence of dreams left her even more lonely than the empty bed did.

She got up and dressed without looking at herself in the mirror. She brushed her hair by running her fingers through it a few times; she shook her head and freed the thick heavy waves that framed her face like heavy drapes. She pushed the hair up and away from the sharp angles of her face, but she neglected to pin it up. Instead, she left it as it was. It hung loose down her back. This ritual was much more comfortable and less time consuming. Ten seconds from now, she can almost hear Henry telling her that she looks indecent, wanton, and raw.

She knows that today she will have to make time to fix her hair to a more suitable fashion before he gets home from work. This adds one more thing to her list of daily tasks. Drink tea, clean the cups, make dinner, fix her hair, pretend, pretend, pretend.

It is the pretending that is most time consuming.

She waits in her room until she is certain Henry has left for work. Forced awkwardness so early in the day requires manners that

Isabelle does not believe she was ever taught, and at 36 years of age, she feels they would be impossible to learn now.

Isabelle eventually hears the front door to the house open and then closes again. She counted to one hundred and fifty, giving Henry time to make it past the front steps and down the street before she felt safe to open the door to her bedroom. She meets the chill of their upstairs hallway and breathes in the stale air that still tastes like last night's lies and grief, now many months aged.

She pretends she is smelling the fresh air of outdoors. There is a moment of realization now, when she understood that it had been well over a month since she has left the house. Her bare feet plod down the hallway, the coolness of the floor against her skin send chills through her body, giving her goosebumps. Her morning walk downstairs before she has had the first cup of her medicated tea, is when she was at her most clear. She sees the house for what it is and what it had become.

It is just a small box, with windows and shadows of sadness lurking behind all the doors and in each of the corners. A sadness that cries for three minutes and is then silent, the cries exist in her version of the world. The one that is ten seconds removed from the rest of them, so naturally, no one else hears this crying or feels the darkness. She can feel the darkness, its fingers as they reach out, they could almost touch her skin if she were not careful.

She walks faster through the parts of the house where the dark lives. She knows due to her neglect that the dark shadows in the far corners have been allowed to grow like weeds and become small sad children. This has happened slowly over the past many weeks. Today the sadness reaches its hand out to her and tugs at her dressing gown as she walks. She imagines that it cries out to her, it wants to be picked up and held against her heart. This darkness wants her to make it a home.

If she turns around now, she will see Oscar, grown now into a toddler. He would walk towards her on chubby and unsteady legs that

34

wobble as if he is walking on a path of crooked stones. She will wonder why it was she thought he had died, and how it was possible that she had not seen him until now. How big he had grown, her little man.

Then she would remember that she lives ten seconds and one lifetime away from him, and he would shrink back into the corner. His shadow would fade and blend into the green silk, walls. He would once again turn back into the darkest of the corner shadows. With no other choice, she would be left to turn her head away from him and continue to walk down the hall.

She always picks up speed as she goes down the stairs. Even as a child she was scared that there would be something reaching out to her. Its spindly fingers knot their way into her long hair. She would feel those little hands tugging against her hair as it hung down her back. She wonders if this is the truth behind wearing your hair up. If it makes a woman less susceptible to reaching fingers that tangle inside of you, pulling you backwards into the dark corners, into ten seconds ago or pushing you into ten seconds from now.

Where is it that she lives when she runs down the stairs in fear?

She got to the bottom of the stairs and she ran towards the kitchen, she took one last glance over her shoulder, expecting to see the shadow child, the little visitor, reaching for its mother.

Not it . . . his.

His mother.

Her.

There is of course nothing behind her; just a bannister that needs polishing and stairs badly in need of a broom. She exhaled in relief as she turned towards the kitchen to see Henry and Mother Minnie sitting at the table. She let out a startled coughing sound. Her breath began to move faster, as if she had broken out into a full sprint, though she is standing still.

35

"Well, well, we were beginning to think you would just sleep all day dear. We know you are tired, but this is a little ridiculous. Oh, and look at yourself, not even dressed, hair undone, running around like a wild thing." Mother Minnie speaks quickly and wears a smile that cuts across her face like a knife, one that is so sharp it makes her mouth look like a garish wound.

"Don't just stand there panting Isabelle, sit down." Henry says this, with a false sense of casualness, the kind that he used to use when they first met her and he would take her on walks, which she often found boring. At the time, she often found herself wondering if boredom with another person was somehow worse than loneliness.

Isabelle sits across the table from them, and Mother Minnie slides a teacup across to her. She can smell the bitter medicine that has added to it even before she takes her first sip. For this one small thing, she is thankful. She takes a tentative sip; she does not care that the water scalds the inside of her mouth and makes her tongue feel like roughed up wood. Almost instantly, her world is back to her slow-motion life, her ten-second divide between her and them. This buffer of time makes her feel safe.

She hears them talking. Yet as she tried to focus her eyes and look at their faces, she sees that they are silent. They continue to stare at her. She looks at them and she hears whispering, she hears these sounds as they creep out of the walls, the echoes of last night's secret meeting between mother and son.

"Am I supposed to guess what this is all about? Is it a game?" Isabelle laughs too loudly at this, and she can feel them shrink away from her as if she is a gun that can fire on its own, even when it is locked away.

Perhaps she is that gun.

"I will have another tea, thank you. The way it was prepared before will be fine." Isabelle's words had begun to move slowly even to her own ears.

36

Henry got up from the table to prepare her second cup. Isabelle could tell he was grateful for the momentary escape. Mother Minnie continued to stare at Isabelle, the smile now wiped from her face, her lips had become pursed so tightly it looked as if everything south of her nose had been wiped away.

She inhales sharply through her nose, and it makes an almost imperceptible humming sound, the absurdity of that noise makes Isabelle smile, and almost laugh. She tries to stifle it by biting at the insides of her mouth to keep the sound from escaping. The seriousness of the moment also feels dreadfully comic. Her mouth twitched a little and she placed her hand up in front of her face, trying with polite desperation to hold herself together. To be serious. To be sane.

Henry walks around to her side of the table and places the teacup in front of her. The cup rattled against the saucer before a small puddle of the liquid splashed onto the tablecloth. They are in that moment no longer 10 seconds divided from each other. Isabelle laughs, and continues to laugh as she looks up at Henry's face. She hopes in that moment, she will see a camaraderie of sorts between them, that he too will be stifling laughter. Instead of humor in his eyes, she sees a coldness, and then is startled again, as she feels his hand connects with her left cheek with a sharp slap.

She looks at him, and she hopes that he can see the betrayal in her eyes. She hopes that the laudanum has not clouded over her emotions to a point that he cannot read them. He has already turned his back on her; his steps are heavy with anger as he walks to the other side of the table, his feet hitting the wood floor with a precision that is almost militaristic.

"Pull yourself together Isabelle." He is rubbing at the palm of his hand as he says this; the feeling of hitting a woman is new to him. She is afraid that once a door like this is opened, it tends to stay open.

"It is becoming increasingly clear to us that you are unwell Isabelle, and we are doing you a disservice if we continue to ignore your behavior." Mother Minnie says this without sentimentality or

37

warmth. Her words feel like the wind, when it howls in off the ocean at night, days before the weather turns bad.

Isabelle sips her tea, in a deliberate manner. She feels her lip begin to swell, and when she licks it, she tastes not only the bitterness of the tea but also the tangy copper of her own blood.

"I'm not unwell. I'm grieving." She says this. Her words are spoken into the almost empty teacup and she can hear them echo back to her repeatedly.

"You're not grieving Isabelle. If you were grieving, you would cry. You do not cry; you do not do anything. You grow stranger by the day, and frankly it's embarrassing, not just to me, and to mother, but you should be embarrassed for yourself." Henry fires these words at her in a rapid pace, too quick for her to be able to reply, her ten seconds that she lives in apart from him had made this impossible. Her mouth cannot possibly move fast enough to form a defense.

"Now, dear, we understand you must feel awful for not being able to hold that baby to term, and not taking better care of yourself while you were pregnant. You probably want to punish yourself, and that is fine. It is almost normal, but you are not just punishing yourself, you are punishing Henry. How do you think he feels having to see you like this? Frankly, you are being selfish; this is not about you Isabelle."

"But it should be," Isabelle whispered this into the teacup in a musical way. She lets the notes bounce back to her before she took another slow sip.

Mother Minnie slams her hand on the table. It makes a similar sound to Henry's palm against Isabelle's cheek from a few minutes before. Isabelle wonders if this is because they have a similar shape hand, a fact that she has never noticed before. Her eyes study Minnie's hand where it rests like a cat ready to pounce on the table. Then Isabelle's eyes move to Henry's hand. He is still gingerly rubbing it, soothing himself over the trauma of his hand 'having' to hit her.

Isabelle hears Minnie whisper to Henry almost under her breath. "It's this strange off-putting behavior that probably made her family give her away to begin with."

"My parents died from Yellow Fever when I was ten, you know that. They didn't give me away . . ." Isabelle looks to Henry now, in hope that he will say something comforting.

"Yes, but you had other relatives that could have stepped in . . . none did. You have always been a bit difficult darling. I looked past it for years; I told myself and everyone that would ask that it made you unique. *Special*." Henry chuckles a little, but the laugh ends in disappointment. "Now this situation with the baby has made you behave, in such a way that is not acceptable." He says this, and then pauses, and finally looks into her eyes. "We know how tired you are."

"I've told you Henry, I'm not tired"

"We think It's best dear if you go away for a rest for a little while. When you come back you will feel so much better, you will be a whole new woman." With those words, the sharp knife of Minnie's smile once again cuts across her face.

"You're sending me away? Am I going to an asylum?" Isabelle feels the severity of this threat, and the noose tightening around her neck. The ten seconds that separates them growing much longer, until it is no longer just seconds, it is a lifetime. It is miles. It is walls in a room with a locked door.

"No, my goodness why would you think that dear? No, we are sending you to a hotel, for the summer, to rest, to heal. It seems awfully paranoid of you to think that Henry and I would trick you into going to an institution, some sort of horrible asylum. Though frankly, I can see why you would be sensitive to things like this, with your upbringing and all." There has always been a subtle blossoming meanness to Mother Minnie, but throughout this conversation, it seems to have bloomed into a full rose of hate. Its petals spread for all to see, with the tips of each turning black with a creeping rot.

"I didn't grow up in an asylum, I grew up in and orphanage." Isabelle whispers into her empty teacup. She waits for those words to echo back to her, the seconds stretch through time, and just when she is about to give up hope, her words find their way back to her. They sound like a different version of herself, the, *her* that is more than ten seconds behind in this conversation. How many versions of her live in this house, all just a few seconds apart? She moves her head around the room looking for herself, hoping that if she moves her head in just the right angle that she will find the version of her that is *well*. Isabelle would do whatever it took to make *her* sit here, and convince Henry . . . convince Henry . . . convince . . .

Suddenly she is confused, more so than she should be. They are right she has grown tired. She raises her head, peeling her eyes away from the empty teacup. She looks across the table expecting to see their faces, both expectant and confused.

The table is empty, the light in the kitchen is warm, and when she looks at the clock it is almost 2pm. Isabelle realizes she has been sitting there for some time, that Henry has long since left for work, and Mother Minnie had probably grown impatient with her and left.

Or perhaps, none of it really happened.

She gets up from the table and walks to the teakettle that has long grown cold in the hours since morning. She looks out the window over the kitchen sink; the street seems unusually quiet, as if the entire world has fallen into their own deep and dreamless state.

She is the dream that they have ceased having. She is the ghost in this house on a hill, the motherless child and the childless mother.

Chapter 5

Isabelle would like to believe she was on her best behavior in the days following the incident of the "summer hotel," but she knows those are lies. She knew that she was being punished because she stopped pretending to care about the façade or normalcy of her new life. The teacups lined the surfaces of the house; their little graves abandoned. She could almost imagine the tea leaves and stains at the bottoms of the cups, as if they were weeds growing over little untended gravestones. She thought of the humble markers of her own family from long ago. They now seemed lost and forgotten.

During the day if she found herself in need of another teacup, she would just pick one of the dirty ones from a bookshelf and use it. This she realized was a much more efficient use of her time. She wondered as she danced on the edge of this new normal, how much of her 36 years of life was wasted cleaning something, just to dirty it again moments later.

Henry would mumble under his breath that if she kept insisting on drinking out of dirty cups that she would likely get sick. Though to be fair, he was the one that was claiming she was sick to begin with, so why not become just what everyone thought she already was. Also, if his worry were indeed genuine, he would have washed the cups as well.

She became tired.

She became in many ways, much more tired than she thought she was.

Isabelle was told she was leaving at the end of the week. She was told to pack up her things. For the life of her, she could not really understand what it was she was supposed to bring to a hotel for the summer. If this was in fact a hotel and she was going on a holiday, it became even more confusing for her. Isabelle had never been on a holiday before, and she found herself mainly fixated on the fact that she should bring a sun hat of some kind. Something to take residence in the currently empty hatbox that sat atop one of the two steamer trunks that she was given to use, *but not to have*, from Mother Minnie.

When Minnie brought the steamer trunk into her room, she was overly dramatic about it. The old woman huffed and wheezed as she pulled it up the steep front staircase. The empty trunk slammed into each stair with a loud hollow thud. Isabelle had asked her a few times if she needed help, or if she would prefer, Minnie could just leave it at the bottom of the stairs until Henry was home. Her Mother-in-law did not want to hear any of it. It was clear to Isabelle that all Mother Minnie wanted was to be the great martyr of the empty luggage.

When she finally managed to wrestle it down the hall and into Isabelle's room, she straightened up with a deep and heavy sigh. She wiped imaginary sweat from her brow as if she were a talentless stage actress and waited for praise to be heaped upon her.

"Thank you, Mother Minnie." Isabelle said with a sweetness in her voice that was so overly saturated is sounded like poison, even to herself. "I don't know how it would have been possible for me to be sent away with only one trunk, I'm very grateful for the second one."

The next day Minnie deposited the infamous hatbox but did not wait for praise or poison before turning quickly and leaving Isabelle once again alone, with her empty travelling companions. Isabelle was in the secret parts of her heart, a bit excited about the prospect of being on a Steamer Ship, as it brought her almost an hour out into the ocean to an Island she had never heard of until just days ago.

42

Dagger Island.

Though Isabelle had grown up here in Portland, Maine and had seen the tides ebb and flow from almost every place she had ever lived, she had never been further into the Atlantic than roughly shin deep. She had never been on a boat that took her out into the sea. She could hardly imagine the possibility that she and the boat itself could sink to the bottom of the ocean floor. That if that were to happen, that there would be more water than she could fathom on top of her. The weight of it would buffer her from a now unknown and foreign world that lived thousands of feet above her head.

The smallness of her life thus far made her feel both ashamed, and relieved. Ashamed that she had become nothing more than a glorified washer woman somehow turned into a wife, and relieved because she never had to fail at becoming more than that.

On the Friday evening before she was to depart early the next morning, Henry came home from work with an elegant sun hat. It had a deep emerald green ribbon that matched the interior of the hatbox perfectly. It was as he called it, a 'Bon Voyage Gift,' but as Isabelle still lived in a world ten seconds removed from him, she said thank you, but it was too late. She heard the door to their room close quietly and then heard his footsteps receding down the hall. They grew less fearsome as they retreated, like a storm going out to sea.

He returned to her room several hours later, after she had failed to go downstairs prepare a final dinner together before her summer sabbatical. He brought with him a few slices of toasted bread with orange marmalade and a cup of her dark and bitter medicinal tea. He placed them on the edge of the small table nearest 'her side' of the bed.

The cup, she could tell was washed clean before the tea was added. It was in this small gesture that she felt herself soften towards him. The clean cup and the toasted bread that was both burned on the edges and cold in the center was a more gentle way of him showing affection than she had perhaps ever seen from him even when they first met.

She took a few sips of the tea and closed her eyes. She felt her lids burn as she did this, and knew it would take considerable effort for her to open her eyes and focus them once again on Henry's doughy moon shaped face. She was nearing the end of what seemed to her like an endless day that started many months ago with three minutes of crying and is only coming to a dull end at this moment. She had been sitting on the edge of the bed, staring at the shadows as they danced their way across the wall.

She felt the other side of the bed sink under his weight, and he once again took his place across that divide. He was fully dressed, save for the shoes, which had thunked onto the floor moments before like rocks in a dried out well. It broke the silence that surrounded them like unexpected thunder on a sunny day.

Henry lay next to her on top of the sheets, staring up at the ceiling; his face seemed to be taking it all in, as if for the first time. This was the first visit back to a room he had all but avoided for the past months. His breath was shallow and tense, and when Isabelle finally relaxed herself next to him on the bed, she could see out of the corner of her eye that he was biting at his lips repeatedly and fidgeting with his fingers. He was winding his hands over and over as if he were a worrying father, and not a concerned husband.

"I am not the enemy here." He whispered at her without daring to move his head to see her.

Isabelle rolled over onto her side to get a better look at him. She stared at him; unspeaking, hoping to see his veneer crack and honesty begin to ooze out. It did not happen.

"You should be thanking me. This could have been much worse for you." He pauses, awaiting her heartfelt thanks, but he is met instead with a silence that is almost tangible. "This, it was the best compromise I could get for you, for us." He turned to her now, just his face. He glanced at her for a moment and went back to staring at the ceiling.

"Did she want me gone for good?" Isabelle asks, even though she already knows the answer. What she did not expect was the hurt feelings that went along with it. She thought she was too numb to feel anything. She was wrong.

"Yes, she thought it would be much easier for me to divorce you if you were shown to be unstable." With these words, Henry rolled over onto his side facing her. His face was about ten inches from her. The only thing that separated them on the bed was this new betrayal.

The pale stained whispers and shadows on the mattress and sheets from One that seemed impossible to climb as if it were slicked over with ice. They were left with little to say, and only the ability to stare at each other from what seemed like an insurmountable emotional distance. When Henry spoke to her it sounded like he was whispering from the end of a long hallway. She heard his words clearly enough, though they seemed like they were meant for someone else.

"You can't have children now; do you understand that?" Though it was a question, the terse way in which Henry said the words made Isabelle understand it was more a statement of fact. It was one, that she had suspected, yet the doctor had never bothered to tell her.

"Yes, yes, I think I understood that. I mean, I never . . . I haven't . . . ." She seemed to stutter her words. "I haven't thought about another child, not yet . . ." Isabelle tried to say these words with strength . . . she failed. Was there any right thing for her to say? She did not know.

"I need to be able to have children Isabelle. I . . . I mean she . . . I mean . . . we . . . we do not think it would be fair in the long run for you to stop me from doing that. I'm sure you agree." This time the inflection in his voice was all wrong, the last part of his words, meant to be a statement came out as a question. His pitched raised a little at the end.

"What am I supposed to do here? There is what I need, what I want and sometimes it does not matter if those two things are different, right. It doesn't matter for you, and it certainly doesn't matter for me?" He pauses and waits, but he is met with silence. He sees a tear finally run screaming from Isabelle's left eye, and for a moment, she can tell that he believes he has finally broken her. He thinks that she will crack, pull at her hair, and beg for the hospital. But instead, she wipes the tear away silently and continues to stare at him, unblinking.

"When I look at you right now, what do you think I see? I see a ghost; I see a shadow of something. You, you are not my wife, when I look at you, I do not see my wife. I try. But when I close my eyes and think about it, you are not, *NOT* my wife." He says this as if he has had a profound realization about the world. Isabelle looks at him, she sees that he is sad, or at the very least playing the role of Pierrot. She sees his pantomimed sadness, but she does not feel it.

He is mourning what he thought his life would be, but he is not mourning her, or their son. He has already moved past the three minutes of family, and their lifetime of nothing. He is only mourning himself and now, she hates him for that.

"So, we are left with this, you will go away for the summer, and you will try and heal. I hope for your sake you do. I am not sure though to be honest that if it really makes a difference. I mean, I want you to be well, but the fact of the matter is it would be easier for me if you were not." Henry pauses, stares at her, his eyes trying to be intense, but merely staring out blankly at her until the pressure builds between them and he looks away. A flash of fear and pity move across his face. He stares back at the ceiling and mumbles to himself, "This is incredibly difficult for me, don't make it worse."

"You're right. I'm sorry." Isabelle says this as a deep hateful giggle begins to build in her throat. "I should be thankful . . ." She can barely get the last part out before a deep laugh comes out of her like sickness kept in too long.

Henry ignores this and pretends to cough and clear his throat to muffle the sounds of her emotions as they swing from highs to lows like an orchestra as it warms up before a symphony.

"I'm sleeping here tonight, but don't worry I won't touch you unless you allow it but I need to get used to sleeping here again now that you will be gone. I mean, away, now that you will be away." Henry's voice shatters a little at the end, but then he quickly glues himself back together, and rolls back over onto his side to face her.

"I would rather you not touch me." Isabelle says this, but in that moment after she finished her sentence, she sees the disappointment crawl across his face, as if she has wronged him yet again. "But I won't fight you, and I won't say no, if *touching* me is what you feel you need to do, if it would make things easier for me to return home to some kind of life, then you can do what you need to do." She pauses, and finally says, "I won't say yes, but I won't say no." With those words, a few more tears fall from Isabelle's eyes, which until tonight, had not wept.

She cried a little harder when she saw that he was undoing the buttons of his pants and taking them down. She finally sobbed, after months of numbness, as he rolled on top of her and pushed himself inside her still wounded body.

She had only earlier that week finally stopped bleeding.

The act itself did not last long. He was done almost before she could imagine it all away. He looked at her as if she were a disgusting thing, and then rolled over and fell asleep. His socks and dress shirt from the day were still on.

She laid there in her bed, the place of love, death, loneliness, and rape. She was awake until this final night became the paranoid, frightening, and almost demonic hours between three am and five am on what could be her last morning in the place she thought was home.

When she finally rose from the bed, she opened the trunks that were left near the door of their room. She placed all of her belongings in them. Her material life consisted of mainly plain clothes, in beiges and sullied whites, and one Sunday dress in a pale robin's egg blue. She included several books that she had hidden away, her favorites by Tennyson, Byron, and copies of Poe, she held the bible in her hands and contemplated it for a few minutes wiping the dust off it that had grown there for the past months like mold on bread.

She thought better of it and she put it back on top of her bureau . . . all these books, which were so personal to her, had been hidden for years underneath her petticoats in the bottom drawer of her bureau. It felt right to her that they too would travel with her on this summer *holiday*.

The night had not quite become day when she laid herself down in the bed once again. She closed her eyes, and finally, she slept.

Chapter 6

Isabelle woke a little over an hour later as daylight screamed into the world. The sun shone bright, albeit briefly before it was brought to a thundering and violent end by a storm battering itself against the coast and hammering their house with thick rain that sounded like bullets.

She felt a mixture of relief and discouragement at this overwhelming obstacle in the way of her future doom. "Henry, the weather is bad; I don't think the boat will go today." She says this, but it is not until her words trail off into nothing that she understands that she is speaking into the empty echo of her room.

She is alone.

In the one hour she slept, he vanished, like a criminal in the night. She was left there on her soiled sheets, the only witnesses being her two packed trunks and her beautiful hatbox, holding her even more beautiful, but very unwanted hat.

She imagines little Oscar, his small blue body, a complimentary shade to the silk inside that box. The blue tinge to his skin and the deep greens of the silk, they would look like the ocean. She imagined him curled up inside that hatbox and then being smuggled onto the island with her. That would be it, the great joke played on all of them. He was not dead, he never died it was all a mistake.

Terrible grief for no reason; all because no one thought to just open the hatbox, and look inside. See.

But then she remembered she did not have the hatbox then, and he cannot possibly be inside there. She sits up in bed, and as her feet touch the floor the door opens, and Mother Minnie enters the room. A bright placid smile on her face, and in her hands, she holds a small tray. It contains a cup of tea and one untoasted piece of bread, covered in Strawberry jam, which Isabelle cannot eat.

"It's your big day, are you excited for your trip?" Minnie is almost singing this. As she says the words Isabelle can see her eyes darting over the room, imagining the new, younger childbearing shadow wife that will take her place, the one that along with Henry will fill this mausoleum of a house with life, with song with . . .

"The weather is terrible, I'm not sure if we will be able to get there, do the boats run when it's like this . . .?"

Isabelle does not finish her words before Mother Minnie chimes in.

"Oh, don't be ridiculous, of course you can still go, it's not like it is a special boat just for you. You will be on the same one that takes the mail to the Island; they must go. You will be fine!" She says with what Isabelle wishes was false enthusiasm but knows in her heart that it is real. Minnie shoves the tray with the tea and bread in Isabelle's general direction and almost lets it go of it before Isabelle even has her hands on it. Minnie halfway out the door before Isabelle says, "I'm allergic to the strawberry, I can't eat this." The door closes on her words, which are either unheard or uncared for, or maybe it is both.

"Aaaaggghhhhhh" Isabelle screams and throws the plate with the cold and poisonous bread against the door as it swings to a close. "BITCH" she screams, and she knows that it is too late to fight her fight, she has lost, and maybe she lost years ago.

50

Was it when she met Henry, or was it before, when she was just a girl, polishing a bannister for hours in a large house that would never be a home? She takes a sip of her tea and thanks whatever she thinks of as a God that it is dark brown and bitter with the laudanum.

Isabelle dresses herself in the plainest of her clothes, the most unassuming of all her bland browns and white smocks and dresses. She realizes now that she has always been dressed as if she were a blank wall in the orphanage of her youth. She never thought of herself in color, always instead in a faded sepia tone of dust and memory.

She always thought of herself as someone that could fade into nothing in almost an instant, a stain that could be wiped away before it sticks for good. She thinks of the emerald green inside her hatbox, and wishes instead that it were a brilliant blood red.

Chapter 7

The walk to the pier, where Isabelle is to board the boat, takes just under ten minutes. Henry pulls her two trunks on a small cart and Isabelle holds the hatbox close to chest, tenderly like the sleeping child she never held. Mother Minnie walks beside Isabelle, holding an umbrella over Isabelle and trying when she can to sneak herself under its shelter to safety. Minnie makes grousing noises as if all of this is a huge inconvenience for her.

Isabelle does not care about any of it. She does not care about the rain that screams down hard on her face, rain that seems too cold for early summer. Nor does she care for the dark mottled brown mud that slowly begins to climb up her legs and her skirt with each step. No, Isabelle realizes now, that the months of not feeling fresh air on her face and wind against her skin were a punishment she was giving herself . . . and in the short walk to the pier she began to think for the first time . . .

"Maybe I don't deserve punishment."

The rain falls and ricochets off the cobblestone streets like shrapnel. The water beats against all the uneven surfaces and it makes an almost deafening constant roar as they approach the pier. No one hears Isabelle when she says, "It's not my fault that he died."

She realizes she said this a little too quietly, so she says it again louder. She finds her voice somewhere underneath the rain and dirt. "It's not my fault that he died!"

She can tell both Henry and Minnie had heard her this time. Both of their heads made a slight twitch motion. It is something that if you noticed them on the street, you would think they had some sort of palsy and turn your eyes away, almost embarrassed you had seen something you knew they were ashamed of.

Isabelle stops in the road. The hatbox clutched to her lovingly. Minnie got about six full steps before she noticed she wasn't next to her daughter in-law anymore. Henry, much further ahead of them did not notice until Isabelle said again, this time, much louder . . .

"It is NOT MY FAULT HE DIED!"

At this point, the people on the streets began to stop and stare for a moment before they would continue walking. These strangers were pretending not to listen yet all the while; they kept one eye and one ear trained on this family in the road. The ones walking in a sad line, each of them covered in mud, and carrying a woman's belongings like a funeral procession.

Isabelle stands there, the rain assaulting her like small fists in a schoolyard brawl; she accepts them. As she raises her chest, she clutches that hatbox to her, she can begin to feel Oscar's ghost, as it claws his way back from wherever he was. He starts to come alive inside of that hatbox, a small boy, now so full of life. Isabelle knew even when he was born, that he would never wear beige. He would always be a boy in the brightest colors; the emerald green inside this box was a fitting new home for him.

She feels him kicking and squirming inside that box. He is alive now and she holds him close to her now because she never could before. The rain hits her face, the mud on her legs weights her down and gives her strength at the same time.

"IT IS NOT MY FAULT HE DIED!"

She feels the pinching and pulling at her arm even before she is finished shouting. Minnie pulls her under the umbrella, and Henry moves with greater speed towards the pier, towards the boat, towards the new shadow wife not yet painted into the picture.

Isabelle stops walking compliantly and instead she is almost dragged the last ten or fifteen feet towards the ticketing counter. She can hear Henry mumble something at the ticket agent, something about "she won't be too much trouble."

Isabelle stifles the urge to scream out that she wants to be trouble – that she will be…, but Mother Minnie sees her open her mouth to shout and in an instant, her nimble fingers press something into the back of Isabelle's throat. It feels like paper, but it tastes like poison. Isabelle tries to bite down on her fingers to stop her but suddenly everything is slow, and her teeth connect with Minnie's fingers but instead of a bite it is a kiss, it is an almost thank you . . .

Isabelle slows down even more, mentally, and physically. Minnie brings her hand to the side of Isabelle's face in what in normal circumstances could have been seen to an outsider's eyes as a loving gesture. Yet Isabelle feels this for what it is, her own surrender.

Isabelle leans her face into Minnie's hand and for just a few seconds it feels like love, a few seconds after that it morphs into something adjacent to love, and then seconds after that it feels much, much worse. It feels like control. She closes her eyes and leans into her hand, and leans into whatever Henry and Mother Minnie have created for her future, she holds on for a moment, and then she lets go . . .

She opens her eyes a few moments later and she finds herself alone on end of the pier. There is bustling activity behind her, but when looks ahead all she sees is water. She turns her head to see a kind gentleman wheeling her two trunks onto the boat. The umbrella is gone, and the rain has soaked her. It pelted at her skin until it has grown raw, chaffed, and shriveled with the abuses of the morning weather. The hatbox is far too wet; she feels the low-end craftsmanship start to come away at the seams. She feels this in her body, as she leans over to protect the hatbox from the wind and rain. She feels this echo inside of her, as the part of her that is made of only emotion starts to bleed. She feels it when the eyes of the ship porter see her for what she is.

Cold.

Wet.

Alone.

A mother . . . who was not a mother.

A wife . . . who was not a wife.

He moved her bags onto the ship, and then with a gentleness that has never been known to her, took her by the arm. It was the way a grown son would hold onto his elderly, yet still beloved, mother and walked her onto the boat.

"It may be better if you sat inside ma'am, the weather is angry today, and we would hate you to catch a chill before your holiday."

He said this with utmost earnestness, after having looked at her face, where the tears should have left her ravaged, but they had not. He then looked down the length of her body and at her and mud-caked dress and shoes, which were so filthy it looked like she was wearing work boots. She was utterly alone. This kind man had somehow seen all of this and still had the compassion to say that it would be a vacation for her. He gave her the dignity of one final lie.

"Thank you for the offer, but if you could take this," Isabelle hands the young baggage porter, the now weathered and abused hatbox. This thing, an inanimate object that she never thought she could care for had suddenly become dear to her. Somewhere in the far edges of her thoughts, she understood that this box held either the most beautiful hat that she had ever owned, or the ghost of her son. Both things at this lonely moment in her life were precious to her.

He took the hatbox into the interior cabin and placed it alongside her other things. Her belongings lay there quietly abandoned as they leaned against bags of mail that were headed out to the island with her. She thought of all the handwritten letters, all the bittersweet missives sent from far away. She imagined several days from now or sometime early next week that she too would begin to receive letters. She tried hard to imagine the reality of that; what it would look like and how it would feel. The image of her sitting quietly on the edge of the bed, hands shaking as they tore into brittle envelopes to pull out a sheet of neatly scribed paper. She suddenly felt very lonely. She knew already without ever having received a letter before in her life, that the letters she would eventually receive would never quite live up to the romanticism she felt just in hoping for a letter.

She closed her eyes, as the boat began to pull away from the dock. The air on her face changed almost immediately. She cannot be quite certain what caused her tears to finally fall, but they did, just as the sky opened again. The world around her began to weep silently, until the violence of the air around her, filled the sky with screaming wails.

Yes, this was angry weather indeed.

Chapter 8

A few minutes after they left the harbor the air around her turned into an almost milky opalescence of fog. The air was thick, with foreboding humidity that was chilled underneath with a piercing cold. She could see her breath for mere moments before it swam into the fog around her and disappeared. She made a game of it, seeing how long she could see her breath before it faded away. The longest she managed to keep track of her own air, was about three seconds. Often it faded just as she saw it.

She was interrupted on an almost clock-like basis for the first 20 minutes of the ride. Gentleman who 'meant well' repeatedly asked her if she would rather be sitting inside, with a warm cup of tea. She politely declined each time. She preferred instead the company of the weather and the ever-increasing violent rocking of the waves. After months of her tea-laden prison, she could not bear the thought of walls around her right now, nor could she think of drinking another tea, laced with laudanum or not. She believed at this moment that she was done with that polite yet pandering beverage. Had they offered her a touch of warm brandy or whiskey, well that she thought she may have taken them up on. She could almost picture herself, sipping whiskey and laughing loudly while playing a game of cards with these men, gruff like sailors one minute, and polite as postal carriers the next.

She smiled to herself. She almost felt ashamed. There was a moment of joyous freedom for her, even if it was only imaginary. The waves began to nip up over the sides of the boat, splashing onto the sole before rushing back out. Each time this happened, she became more certain that she was the target of this watery anger. She stretched her legs out to their furthest, hoping to feel the cold-water grab at her ankles. The water did manage to make it to the tips of her dirty boots a few times; each one seemed like an invitation to her.

Isabelle had always feared the water. She feared its unpredictable and violent nature, but today, it felt different, it woke something inside of her. She was a dragon that lay long asleep that had woken to roar finally. She stood up with deliberateness and care. The mud that had caked her shoes mingled with the briny seawater and each tentative step felt as if she were about to slip on the iced over cobblestone streets near her home.

She could hear the hail even before she could see it, though it was masked deep within the fog that surrounded her. She heard it almost tear through the air with a roar and then it began to ping like rocks off the ship. As the hail hit the waves, it made an almost deafening sound. It was the all-encompassing roar of the sleeping monster inside of her. It called to her and she allowed herself to roar back at it, screaming almost silently into the wind.

The weather woke up along with her anger. The bolts of lightning were the only things breaking through the fog. She thought she could see something in the distant waves before the light from the strike faded away, leaving a strange blue green hue to the air. That sleeping monster under the water, it stretched its hand out and pulled the electricity down from the sky and into its open gaping maw.

She put her hands on the support beam and pulled herself up, placing her feet on the middle railing. She laced one arm around the beam and with her other hand, she reached out from under the safety of the awning. Her hand stung with the force of the hail; her skin grew so cold it began to feel hot. It seemed to shrink, and shriveled in mere seconds. The hail felt like the wasps that angered after she slammed a door too hard during a seemingly endless summer afternoon when she was younger. She feels the same as those stirred up hornets now that she has nothing better to do than to get angry and find someone to sting.

Her feet seem to slip a little against the railing and she finds herself holding on tight to the post, she almost forgot that her arms could feel this strong. She leans as far forward as she can. She tilts her face up towards the sky and the rain and hail hit her so hard that it almost knocks the breath from her. The strange early summer ice batters against her skin and her throat. It feels like small cold hands pounding against her windpipe, teasing her with breath and then taking it away. The sensations are overwhelming, and she tries to laugh, but water fills her mouth almost immediately so her laugh muffles into a choking cough.

She loosens her grip on the post just a little, leans a few more inches over the railing, she hears a song of terror and freedom someplace deep below the waves. That angry monster feels her and begins to call her home. She leans, she leans, she leans just a little bit more into it . . .

Suddenly, she feels herself almost violently being pulled down from the railing. She turns to look at one of the ship's porters. His arms still wrapped around her waist; she must strain her neck to see him. She expects to find his face filled with concern but she's met instead with a combination of annoyance and confusion. He says nothing to her. His message is clear as he pulls her inside the interior cabin. He pulls her by the arm like a child who has lost her way. He sits her roughly down on a stool near the corner; she is in between strangers' suitcases and bags of lonely letters.

Her fingers reach up and delicately touch her skin, which feels as if it has been pelted raw. Without seeing herself, she knows that the little welts she feels against her exposed skin have turned into a screaming array of stars on a dark night. Isabelle's pale skin will be cracked by morning. She is busy reading her own features as if she is blind and discovering herself for the first time. It is then that she feels a warm cup placed in her hand. It seems so natural, so comforting. She should be thankful.

"Take this, and get your senses together, we're almost there." The voice is gruff and comes from what appears to be a bearded shadow man.

"Do you have anything stronger than this?" She asks this, with the memory of her imagined laughter and card games still so fresh in her head that it could have almost been real.

"No just tea for the ladies, and you should be grateful for it too." This faceless man has already walked away, leaving her alone with another cup of goddamned tea. She reaches into one of the bags of mail, makes a small cave in the center of the pile, and pours the tea in there. She can see that the dark brown liquid has already begin to stain and smear the almost indecipherable handwriting. For whatever reason, she hopes those letters never find their way home.

Chapter 9

The boat began slow down, almost to a glacial pace, as it moved on its steady course towards the island. She stood up quietly and walked to the doorway. She still was feeling her chastisement from before, and like a child, she was afraid to inch her toe over the doorway and into the air for fear of being reprimanded again. She did want to see her first glimpse of the island. She wanted it seared into her memory, her first glimpse of this place that would be her home for the next several months.

She saw rocky edifices that looked like a giant and hunched over gray lady begin to emerge from the fog. She was made of stone and deep green barnacled skin. The rocks seemed to go straight up towards the sky, so her first views of Dagger Island were like looking at a wall. As the ship began to hug the rocky coastline, the rocks grew lower, but not more inviting. They seemed to create dangerous pools and inlets. She felt as if things were watching her, things she could not see. Whether these were gulls or the grundylow she heard of when she was small from her grandmother and later, the other children in the poorhouse, she does not know.

The dock seemed to come out of nowhere, it was a long slender wooden finger, reaching its way several hundred yards out into the sudden stillness of the deep gray of the Atlantic. As the ship finally settled itself, the faceless man walked up to her, he took the teacup out of her hands and pushed her into the center of the room.

"You best stay out of the way for a few minutes until we unload. Mail and bags are first, normal passengers are second, and those staying at the hotel are last." The way his voice changed as he said the word *hotel* made a rock form in Isabelle's stomach. A rock that had not yet been smoothed over by years of ocean waves, this rock was still sharp, and it was almost as if it had been violently placed inside her by a stranger.

Hotel

It was a word that was not meant to instill fear but she saw it in his eyes, as they darted away from her, and she heard it in the lower resonance of his whisper. "Hotel". There was a discomfort there. She could tell he was a man saying one word, when he truly meant another. The type of man when he gets home at night still remembers the haunted faces of these 'hotel guests,' and quickly gives himself the sign of the cross before he pinches his eyes closed in order to forget theirs.

She knew that sound well. She had almost made those same subtle and almost hidden noises often in her life, the many times over the years that she said the word "yes," while screaming the word "no" in her head. She felt it, she felt the word "hotel" the way you hear the silent scream of "no" when a body presses into you and you can feel the phantom hand clasp over your mouth before you scream.

Hotel

Hotel

No Tell

No Tell

Goosebumps grew over her skin, climbing her arms and hiding beneath her still wet dress. Suddenly Isabelle sees herself as everyone must see her, her dress caked with water and mud, hair down, wet and tangled, her face littered with red welts. She shivers in the middle of the room, trying to rub her arms with a ferociousness that would bring the dead back to life.

She looks like a mad woman. She looks tired. She looks perhaps even more tired than she thought she was.

She stood there awkwardly in the middle of the small cramped space. She saw the great care these large men took with bags of letters. She saw these same large men grab the suitcases and hall them onto the dock as if they were bags of coal or reams of wood. It was not until the faceless man put his hands on her hatbox that she made an almost yelp of a sound like a kitten who has his tail pulled on purpose by the meanest of the boys in the neighborhood.

"I could take that if you don't mind." Isabelle whispered the words in her best attempt at politeness and the habit of womanhood invisibility.

Isabelle could see the way he handled this hatbox, as if it meant nothing to him. He of course did not understand the small delicate beauty that lay inside of there, a sleeping sun hat for her happiest days, and underneath that, the sleeping child who had only been alive three minutes. The latter was for her worst days.

"One less thing for me to do, thank you Miss, we are almost finished clearing out. You can take this and head down to the head of the dock. The *hotel manager* should be there, or one of his nurses, I mean maids . . . someone will meet you there." Again, his eyes looked down, lingering for a moment too long on her breasts, and then with greater sadness on the muddied bottom of her dress.

Isabelle whispered a plaintive, "Thank you" but it went unheard and uncared for.

She cradled this hatbox close to her, the cardboard and ribbon had grown tattered and flimsy in the weather. Even though they were safely inside the boat, the rain and fog had been invasive like vines that ruin a yard or back porch, making an already too modest home feel even more claustrophobic.

She stepped onto the dock, which she could feel moving and swaying with the water under her feet. It made her feel dizzy and unsettled as if she was waking from an afternoon, all too medicated nap. The rain still fell at an unrelenting but seemingly less violent pace. The size of the drops themselves seemed to be smaller, and finer, like silk. She tried to hunch over the hatbox, forgetting for a moment that it was in fact just a box, and not poor Oscar, three minutes old and gone blue all too soon.

She thought of that pretty sunhat inside of that box, and she knew that was a hat never meant for someone like her. No, a waifish thing, with almost white blond hair, should wear it as she laughed and walked with abandon on a sandy boardwalk. Admirers lagging behind her like a ship's wake.

Isabelle would never be that girl. At the best, Isabelle had only ever hoped to be the too tall maid, or chaperone who walked ten feet behind laughter her entire life. Still, she had the hat now, and out of everything in her very sheltered life, this hat felt real. She walked gingerly along the dock, which seemed to stretch out in front of her, a distance that seemed as if it would take lifetimes to traverse.

It was not until she was at least three quarters of the way towards land that she could see two figures waiting for her. She was thankful upon seeing them, that they did not appear to be doctors, or medical professionals. There were no white coats to speak of, instead, they were both dressed very funereally, which to be honest, was a little more reassuring for Isabelle; a woman who had over the course of her life, attended seven funerals, and only one wedding, her own.

She found herself slowing down as she approached them. Taking her shriveled and still wet hands and running them through her thick and dark nettled hair. Making herself seem at least in the slightest way, a 'touch more presentable.' She could almost hear

Mother Minnie's voice, filled with recrimination and gin, coated with a smile that never met her eyes.

"Hello" Isabelle said first in hopes of appearing friendly. She realized too late that they had not heard her. Her awkwardness caused her almost to curl in on herself, protecting of all things. She focused on the hatbox, which was filled with the ghosts of who she was and who she hoped to be.

As she got a little closer she again gave a more lackluster shout out to her new companions. "Hello . . ."

They did not respond, with the exception that she saw a wave of fear wash over the 'maid's' face. She was a small girl, made mostly of freckles. The girl stepped back two large paces before Isabelle was even in a six-foot radius of them.

"They didn't tell us she was sick, not like that," the girl said, and Isabelle could hear the chimney soot in her voice.

Before Isabelle could say anything, the girl continued, "Look at her, her face and hands she has measles. I'd know it anywhere; it killed my two baby brothers."

The way she said it made it sound more like "broffers" rather than brothers, Isabelle thought to smile, thinking how far this girl has come.

"No, no, no measles, at least nothing was said to us about that." The man, the 'hotel manager' said this while also stepping just a few more feet out of Isabelle's small orbit.

"Ma'am . . . are you sick?" He seemed to shout this, as if whatever were happening on her skin had somehow made her ears invalid.

"No, no I'm not sick . . ."

"But your face Ma'am, you seem to have a rash of some kind . . ."

"No, no, I was out on the deck and it was hailing. It felt like rocks against my skin . . . I'm sensitive, the least thing will make it turn red." Isabelle paused expectantly, waiting for a dawning of realization to break on their faces. She was met with nothing.

Just silence.

The small freckled maid takes an additional step backwards, while leaning into her male companion and in the type of whisper that is meant to be heard, "I can't abide by measles sir, you know that. We should not risk it; we should send her back with the outgoing mail. We can burn her things if we have to."

And in a whisper that should never have been heard over the ocean waves, the silver haired manager leans too closely to his companion and says, "They've already paid. We need to take her; we can put her somewhere . . . it would be too much work to give the money back. We're meant to keep her for four months . . ."

And there it is; Isabelle hears it. It is her sentence, her punishments for not crying, for taking the tea that was given, for being barren, for being old.

Four months.

Ample time for Henry to instill someone else in her place, a shadow wife, young, fertile, and naive enough to think it is normal to scream *no* in her head while saying, "yes" with her voice.

Chapter 10

She walked roughly ten paces behind them. The young maid, whom the older gentleman referred to as Petal, refused to carry Isabelle's belongings for fear of 'measles.' Isabelle struggled with the two large bags, dragging them behind her as if they were a wagon filled with bones in an old churchyard. Not trusting the older gentleman, Doctor, *hotel manager*, she was not sure, to care for her hatbox, she tucked it under her right arm. She tried desperately not to crush it out of clumsy strength.

The walk form the dock to the hotel was slippery and steep, and though she struggled with the bags and keeping her footing on the muddied path, Isabelle felt a sense of accomplishment when she managed to make it to the top of the hill. Looking down towards the ocean, the fog still blanketed the rocky coast. The ship, which she knew still lay dormant in the harbor, was all but invisible. With its invisibility, the ship, and the rest of the world she knew before today began to fade into obscurity and memory.

Dagger Island was a mere 15 miles off the coast of Portland Maine, but it may as well have been in another world. She had heard tell growing up, of a grisly murder that took place out here in the early 1700's. She knew that the supposed murderer had killed his whole family and two of the servant women. Only the gardener had survived. The murderer had then rowed back to Portland in a small skiff in the deepest part of a New England Winter Storm . . . this was not something she could imagine. The thought of being in a small wooden boat, weather attacking you alongside the water through the night, a person would grow exhausted almost immediately. Their hands would be tired, chaffed, and wounded raw by the air and water. It did not seem possible that someone would want to kill someone badly enough to go through the torment to themselves afterwards.

Frankly, he should have been allowed to get away with it, on sheer gumption alone.

She said that once to Henry when they were chatting by the fire one night, whispering and giggling like children talking about all things gruesome and lurid. "If he was willing to row through the night in the storm, they should have let him get away with it." She had laughed and sipped at her warm brandy.

Henry had looked appalled. "Izzy, you can't mean that. He was a monster; he chopped people up with an Ax."

"Don't you ever wonder why he did it? There had to be a reason, people do not just chop each other up for nothing. Then he risked his own life. He had to of thought it was worth it."

Maybe it was the brandy that night, or the darkness. The way they both danced with the firelight. It made her feel a momentary lapse in her daily repression. She let a bit of darkness come out of her, and she liked it.

Isabelle is lost in that old memory, the strange comfort of it tugs her out to sea and pushes her back again, almost violently against the jagged rocks of her present state. She does not even notice that they have left her there; standing at the bottom of the stairs leading into this summer hotel until she turns around and all that surrounds her is fog.

She pushes the heavy doors open with her back, still dragging her own "contaminated" belongings with her. She turns to see a large foyer; its floor is heavy and dark. A collection of small and medium sized Oriental Carpets had been scattered under some of the furniture.

Their deep burgundy and royal blues gave the auspicious and stern looking room a sense of bohemian warmth that it would have otherwise been lacking. There were some guests lingering in the lobby as well, and reading books under the strange greenish hues that the oil lamps gave off in the darkness.

It seemed almost as if it were a real hotel.

"Let us get you upstairs to your room, you can come down in the morning and we can get you situated. You must be tired. We can send up some tea for you." The older gentleman that had been her escort earlier said, as he came out from behind the large desk at the corner of the room.

"Oh, It's alright, I'm not very tired, it's only early afternoon," Isabelle said.

"Oh well, of course your tired, don't be ridiculous. Sometimes we are more tired than we think we are. Isn't that right Petal?" The gentleman said this, calling once again to Petal and bringing her back into the fold.

"You're right Mr. Hughes. You should listen to him Ma'am; sometimes we are more tired than we think we are." The young woman smiled, showing her teeth in a not altogether friendly way; she looked more like a stray dog, desperately wanting love, but also fearful and strange from being left alone too long.

"Petal, you will show Mrs. Baker to her room. Why don't we put her on the third floor, the end of the hallway in the East Wing?" He seemed to pause here, giving Petal a knowing look. "You can ask one of the boys from the kitchen to help with her bags, that way you don't strain yourself with them. Mrs. Baker, is as you can see too tired to manage them any longer."

"Of course, Sir that would be the best room for her, and you are right, she does look very tired." Petal whispered the last part, as she left them to go and fetch some help for the bags.

"You will find the East Wing to be quite pleasant. The morning light is very refreshing, though it is a bit drafty on that side of the building, so we will send one of the boys up with an extra blanket for you. The hot tea will help as well." Mr. Hughes paused and cleared his throat before continuing. "Breakfast is served in the sunroom at 7:00am; it's that large room right through there," he said while gesturing towards a large room that seemed to wrap around the outer edges of the building, like a veranda. "After breakfast tomorrow I will send for you and we will get properly acquainted. My goal is to make you as comfortable as possible here, and get you back to feeling rested and healthy, get you back to normal. Good as new." He smiled awkwardly; all the while, his eyes remained sad.

Even Mister Hughes did not believe what he was saying.

"Thank you, Sir; I look forward to my stay here." Isabelle said this, and though she could taste the lie in her mouth as she said it, she said it, nonetheless. She could not quite cope with the prolonged eye contact, so instead turned her eyes down towards the floor. She noticed that she had left a puddle where she stood, the saltwater and mud swam together on the hardwood floor. The greenish light made it all look a bit gruesome, and for a briefest of moments she felt herself bleeding again, she heard three minutes of crying. It seemed so real it was almost dizzying.

She lifted her head, and cleared her thoughts, as Petal approached.

"Alright, let us head upstairs. You can leave these things here, and a boy will bring them up. I know you say you are not sick Ma'am and I do want to believe you, but we cannot take any risks here on an Island, especially right before summer. So, I would ask you kindly not to touch the bannister on the stairs, or anything in the hallway, just in case."

"Of course, Petal, I don't want to make things any more difficult for you, or for myself." Isabelle tried to sound nonchalant and conversational. As if, she and Petal were two friends, sharing
72

neighborhood gossip. "Petal is a very unusual name; it's beautiful, you're very lucky." Isabelle tried to keep the charade of camaraderie going as they walked up the flights of steep almost never-ending stairs.

"Oh, no, that's not my name. That is just what Mister Hughes calls me. My name's Daisy, so I guess he thinks he is being clever by calling me Petal. I hate it, and I have told him that, but he calls me that anyway. There is nothing I can do about it. I think it is more for him than me. I've always hated nicknames."

Isabelle felt a deep sickening feeling inside of her, already understanding that Mister Hughes would be the type of man to call you dearie, and hug you at family gatherings just a little too long, his hands moving down your body in a way that felt predatory and exploratory. The type of man who would kiss you on the cheek, just a little too close to your mouth and you would have to find a delicate way to wipe the moisture away from your face before you would gag.

They wound their way up the stairs, and down a long sparse corridor towards what seemed like the most remote part of the "East Wing." The rooms they passed all had their doors open and seemed to be unoccupied. The rooms were sparsely decorated. White clean linins and white thin blankets decorated the twin beds. Few rooms had a small writing table by the windows; others had empty bookshelves. All rooms had a small vase holding one pink tulip.

"Here we are then." Daisy gestured into the room at the farthest point of the hallway. "None of the doors have locks on them, and we mainly keep the doors open anyway. You can close your door at night or in the afternoon if you are having a rest. You won't find anyone coming all the way down here to bother you Ma'am, so you don't need to worry. Men are in the West Wing, and there are not too many people at all up here on three. Not this early in the season, we do not allow children here, so it will be quiet. You won't have to become needlessly upset with the sound of a baby crying."

73

Petal, or Daisy, said all of this without thought, and Isabelle assumed that she was in fact just a maid and not a nurse, and had not seen any information about Isabelle's 'case' before now.

"The boys will come up with your bags in a few minutes and I've instructed one of them to bring you a bowl of hot water and a pitcher, so you can get yourself cleaned up. Most of our guests don't come down for dinner on their first night here, so I will send up some broth and bread for you." Daisy paused, and turned to leave the room, but stopped herself, as she got closer to the door. "I can try to find an extra sweet for you as well; we might have some biscuits, or maybe a piece of the lemon cake from breakfast. It shouldn't be too dry yet . . . and about earlier. I am sorry, I can see your skin is looking better already, I shouldn't have assumed you were sick, and I shouldn't have made this situation worse for you Ma'am. I am sure whatever reason you are here is hard enough." Daisy did not smile during this last part. She said it with a solemnity that made her seem like a child with sad and knowing eyes.

"Thank you, Daisy, and you can call me Isabelle."

"That is sweet of you Ma'am, but if you don't mind it's probably better if I stick with Ma'am. I found it's easier for me in the long term if I don't get attached to any of you here. It hurts less."

Yes, poor Daisy, so incredibly young, and so very old.

Once Daisy had left the room, Isabelle found that she was at a loss for what to do. What could she do? She looked around the room, at its stark cleanliness. It was a tantamount opposite to Isabelle's current state. She knew full well that she could not sit on the bed, or the small-upholstered chair that watched her diligently from the corner of her room. She felt just by standing there, that she was soiling the air around her. She scraped her feet together. The mud that had caked them earlier was now turned to a sandy claylike texture, which was flaking onto the floor in small piles. Her immediate thought was that she should not have made such a mess of things so soon.

She was on her hands and knees pushing the dirt under the bed and into the heating vent when two young boys entered with her bags. A third seemingly much younger boy entered behind them, holding a washbasin of warm water and some small towels.

The three boys deposited her belongings and placed the warm water on the table by the window. Isabelle tried to push herself up off the floor in a dignified and graceful swoop. Seeing as she was neither of those things, she felt awkward and heavy, almost like a wild and cumbersome creature rising before them. She was the sea-monster, the grundylow from her youth; her deep fears of the water, coming to life, becoming her . . .

"Thank you." She paused, knowing that if this were a real hotel that these boys would expect her to give them money. She of course, was sent from her home with nothing. She was unable even to pretend for a moment that this was a true summer holiday. The sort of place she dreamed of as a girl.

The three boys nodded politely and left the room without a word. The smallest one, made it about halfway down the long corridor before he sprinted back and closed her door. The sound was heavy and immediate, and made Isabelle think of a cell door closing. She looked around the room, the pale white walls, the crispness of the white sheets, and the cool faded milk of the sky outside her window. It seemed to her, in this room, shadows could not exist.

She had managed to clean herself up and left her muddy boots near the door. She put on a fresh nightdress, something that seemed silly as it was early afternoon. Daisy arrived with a small pot of tea, the promised lemon cake and some toasted bread and butter. Isabelle was barely able to finish any of it, as she began feeling a hazy rush of sleep begin to envelop her. It crept in her window, which was open just a few inches. This overwhelming exhaustion came in with the fog and weather.

As she lay her head down on the pillow, she tried to remember if the tea had tasted like creeping bitterness as it did at home. She reached for the teacup, hoping to trace her finger on the bottom of the cup, wondering if it had the filmy slime of medication coating the bottom. Her hand never made it there; she fell into the nothing somewhere along the way.

Chapter 11

Isabelle was startled awake by a brisk rapping on her door, and for a few moments after she opened her eyes Isabelle was unclear on exactly where she was or worse yet . . . when she was. She sat up, her muscles were stiff, and her bones made deep creaking sounds like wood settling in a damp hallway. She had laid in the same position for hours and as she stretched, her body felt unused and logy. The sky outside her window was still a similar milky color, but she could tell that there was a yellow hue starting to spread out underneath it all. It was morning and she had somehow slept through the night.

She looked to her right and her bleary eyes focused on the teacup that was still there on the table near her bed. She remembered the tea and wondered if there would be a little something added to all of her meals and drinks. Something to keep her sleeping, something to get her rested.

The rapping on the door happened again and she could hear Daisy, in a low and serious voice say, "Ma'am I thought I ought to wake you. You were probably so tired yesterday that you did not set the clock next to your bed. Breakfast is starting in a few minutes and then you will have your meeting with Mister Hughes. Ma'am? Are you awake Ma'am? I don't want to open your door if you aren't decent . . ."

"I'm awake Daisy. Don't worry I will be down in a few minutes." Isabelle was barely finished her sentence when she heard Daisy's footsteps retreating down the hallway. Her steps echoing off the walls like stones thrown down a well that had long ago run dry. She realized she had forgotten to ask Daisy a question, so she darted out of the bed, feeling the room swim around her, swirling for a moment and the edges of her vision going dark before quickly returning to normal.

Isabelle flung the door open and it banged against her wall loudly. It sounded ferocious and unexpected, like thunder on a sunny day; a sound so unexpected that it was thrilling in its force. "Daisy, I did have a question," Isabelle's voice was louder than she had ever remembered it being, even during Oscar's birth.

"Yes Ma'am?"

"I was wondering if it would be alright if I wore my hair down. Or is it mandatory that it be pinned up?"

"Oh, Ma'am I think if it is brushed neatly and nicely there shouldn't be a problem with it being down. It shouldn't be too much of a distraction to the other guests here. I will let you know if I hear otherwise though." With that, Daisy gave a curt nod that almost sunk into a small curtsey before turning and with haste made her way down the hallway to the stairs.

Isabelle felt for the first time that this may indeed be a holiday, if not for herself, at least for her long dark hair. After getting herself ready, she left her room, remembering the rule of keeping her door open. Though this was not her home, she felt somehow that it would expose her truest self and show these strangers the place in which she slept, the place where she dreamt. She left the room after pulling the sheets up and hiding the indentation that her body made in the night. She remembered the soporific nature of her sleep last night and knew there were no lingering memories or dreams hiding in the corner of that room for others to see. Not yet.

Her stomach began to tumble, like fireflies in a jar before they beat themselves against the sides and turn into strange glowing stains. She was nervous, and though she felt strange admitting it to herself, she was also excited.

As a child, she went from her parents' home, to the almshouse. Then she went from the almshouse to Henry's house. She felt her whole life was spent belonging to people who only thought of her as a burden. Though here she was still under someone else's care, she felt for the first time that she was becoming someone new. She no longer had to be an orphan, a wife, a mother of something small and dead, or a lonely witch in a house on a hill, here, she could be something else. She could be something real, solid, made form stone before it was chiseled away into an object meant for someone else eyes.

Her footsteps echoed and sang down the long corridor and it sounded foreign to her. The pattern and meter of her steps sounded like a heartbeat gone awry after eating too much salt on a day that started out too cold and grew too hot. As she got closer to the wide berth of the stairway that led down to her new life, at least for the next four months, she heard and felt her steps grow more even. She was steadier on her feet in this strange place, more than she had even been in her life, as she knew it before now.

The sound her footsteps made came back to her, less like a whisper from a ghost and more like a kiss on her cheek for courage. She felt these echoes the way most people at some point in their lives felt parental love. Once she arrived at the bottom of the stairs, she turned around once again to see the large doors that opened themselves to the wraparound veranda. She saw that the sky was now a warm yellow hue from the east that was spreading out over the water, inching closer to the island.

As the fog from yesterday and the anger of the world around her faded into complacency and acceptance, she felt herself falling in love with the morning sky. The pale yellow grew stronger in its marriage to the steel gray of the cold and the all too turbulent water.

She stood there for what seemed like forever. She was only disturbed by the sudden clearing of a gentleman's throat.

"If you're confused Ma'am, about where breakfast is served, it's right through here. I could show you if you needed assistance." Isabelle turned her head, she half-expected to see the dowdy Mister Hughes, but was instead caught off guard by a much younger man. He was not as young as the "baggage boys" from yesterday were, though it seemed he could not have been much older than nineteen. His skin bore the scars of tortured adolescence, and seeing the scars on his face, Isabelle could almost hear the cruel laughter of girls as they passed him on the street. He was a tall and almost gangly young man, his shape bearing more resemblance to a heron, rather than a man. She looked at him with intent to answer, but he looked down very quickly before she was even able to meet his eyes. He scraped at his throat again and in a half mumble and jerky motion with his arms, he pointed towards the breakfast room.

Isabelle walked past him at his position behind the welcome desk, and she could hear his breath stop as she passed him. As if, he had been for some reason stopping himself for inhaling any bit of the essence of her.

The *infection* of her. She had to be imagining that.

She reached her hands up to feel her skin, to make sure the raised red welts from yesterday's weather were not still scarring her usual all too pale features. Her skin felt fine. She had not seen a mirror since yesterday, so she could not be sure that she appeared on the outside to be 'normal.' She used her hands to tame the long black tresses of her hair once again, as her hair hung down heavily against her back.

She entered the room, the breakfast room. She saw on the wall what seemed to be a friendly sign decorated by children. "Welcome to the sunroom, sit where you are welcome."

She turned herself around in place a few times, making herself a bit dizzy as she went. She realized that a little less than half the tables were occupied with guests. Most people there sat at tables alone, but there were a few that seemed grouped together, less out of camaraderie and comfort, and more in deterrence. The safety of their numbers would allow the sanctity of their group to hold true, even when there were newcomers.

As her eyes scanned the tables, the sun began to break free of a cloud. It made the room seem to grow unnaturally bright and warm almost in almost an instant. She felt as if she was an orchid in a greenhouse, a rare sort of thing that could only exist in a very particular and special circumstance. She would be the type of flower that would not be beautiful to a person's eyes. Instead, she would be the type that seemed odd and had an almost rotting death smell if you got too close. A thing that would only be considered beautiful to someone fond of peculiarities, a flower that glowed white with fear in the moonlight, a flower who made a person's viscera scream like a mandrake being pulled from the earth.

Her eyes landed first on a fleshy woman, with a smile that was the easiest definition of happiness that Isabelle had ever seen. She had a feeling of beatific grace that surrounded her, as she smiled like a new mother to child at the large cinnamon roll she held in her hands. There was a purity there, in her adulation that Isabelle had never felt. She was overwhelmed at once with a grotesque desire to stomp over to this woman's table. With her newly found courageous footsteps and knock the pastry form her hand. Let it tumble to the floor. She wanted at once to see the woman's face crumble, as she had to pick dust and hair from her food before placing it back in her mouth.

Perhaps they were all right about her; perhaps Isabelle needed a rest. Perhaps she was more tired than she thought she was. Her eyes kept traveling the room, to all the broken dolls in this large and decorative toy box. None of them seemed to call out for her, the missing doll part, and the missing arm to their well-loved porcelain doll. The one they received as a child that they thought was meant to

81

be played with but was only there as a way for mommy and daddy to scare their girl into obedience.

She chose instead to continue her isolation for today. She took a table that had grown almost uncomfortably warm in this ever-brightening morning light. She sat there, and before she had even finished straightening her skirts, she was given a large tray of food. It contained one cup of coffee, a cup of tea, two eggs cooked far too long, two pieces of toasted bread, the familiar pastry, which was quite the friend to her more robust companion at the neighboring table. She was taken aback by the quickness of the tray's delivery. She stared at it for a moment before lifting her head to thank whomever it was that brought it to her, but by the time she had lifted her head she only saw a hunched over form leaving the room.

The eggs looked like the hard soles of shoes. The same kind that she once heard talk of in the almshouse that people would be forced to boil in order to make it *food* . This process would take the whole day. Afternoon would seep into the late evening, only then would the inedible become 'a meal.' She could hardly bear to look at them, those vile and staring eggs, challenging her to be at her most poor, her most needy.

She reached into her lap and pulled out the linen cloth she had placed there. Shaking it in an almost spastic twitch, she flung it into onto the eggs before they challenged her to be what she once was instead of who she thought she could be. Was she still the poor girl left alone by her family, or was she the sick wife left alone? The napkin lay there, crumpled, and rude. She picked the tea up and out of habit drank the entire thing in three long sips. It lacked the darkness of the licorice-flavored sleep that had become her constant companion over the past many months.

She closed her eyes; she heard three minutes of furtive crying. She felt the sun travel back behind a cloud and come out the other side brighter and angrier. She opened her eyes. She picked the Danish up in her hands, she wanted for a moment to raise her eyes and see the rotund woman at the next table. She wanted that kinship between them both, an unspoken bond, a deep friendship that formed over nothing, laughter, simple laughter. She raised the Danish to her mouth; she smiled and laughed. Her eyes darted up expecting to find her new friend, and all she found was him . . .

Part 2

Love Alters not with his brief hours

And weeks,

But bears it out even to the edge of

doom.

-   Shakespeare, Sonnet 116

Chapter 12

Isabelle was startled to find that laughter had burst out of her, sounding somewhere between a chortle and a cough. Perhaps she was even more startled to find that she was staring at someone else, who was also laughing, holding a Danish. His eyes looked down at the doughy thing in his hand, he looked furtively at the rotund woman, who still sat there smiling in her beautiful innocence. He rolled his eyes in a dramatic and almost mocking way; he stifled a laugh, and let it hide itself underneath a smirk. It was the type of look that feigned happiness but is riddled with sadness born into anger.

They looked at each other for a few seconds, sharing in the joke that was about another person, and Isabelle was not sure what they were laughing at . . . she thought it was the audacity of happiness. She saw that he put his Danish down, almost as if it had offended him. He stood up sharply, his chair making a noise that sounded like angry geese. He walked out of the room without a second glance at Isabelle. It was not until he walked by her table that she saw his collar. He was a priest.

He passed by her table and after he was gone, she thought she could hear the faint cry of a child, screaming for his mother. A sound only muffled due to the hatbox he was placed in before they were both slid under her bed for safekeeping.

She sat for a few moments, picking the Danish, putting only the sticky and almost raw cinnamon parts in her mouth. Leaving the outer bread portions on her plate like the bones of birds killed in the street. Realizing the mess, she had made of her hands; she dipped her fingers in the glass of ice water that was placed next to her. She splashed them around in there, turning the water into a filthy and un-drinkable marsh. She still had her fingers in the glass when Daisy arrived at her table with a simple note, reading "Mister Hughes, office 7:30am."

"Excuse me Daisy, could you tell me what time it is now?".

"Yes, Ma'am it's 7:30." Daisy said this with little thought to the fact that the time written on the note was the very same one. That Isabelle was already late. A thought that made her feel more jittery, and almost flush with fever.

"Daisy, you should have given me the note earlier" Isabelle knew she sounded harsh, as she said these words. She pushed herself up from the table with such force that she knocked over the water glass; it fell against the tea saucer with clumsy and frantic crash. Isabelle wiped her wet hands, still a bit grimy with cinnamon and icing against her dress, leaving smears that looked like she had claw marks running down the front of her, looking like brown stale blood. She wondered if anyone else could hear that baby crying, so quietly form upstairs. The sounds whether real or imaginary, made Isabelle's hands shake with a newfound nervousness. "Could you tell me Daisy where Mister Hughes office is?" Her voice was shaky, and she was almost out of breath, as if she had come back from a long swim in cold water.

But Isabelle could not swim, of course. It was a silly comparison.

"It's right through the door Ma'am and then go down the hallway on the left, his door will be open. I can take you there if you like after I clean this up." Daisy looked down at the spilled water, she watched as it slowly dripped onto the floor, with small pieces of cinnamon debris in it. The icing made the water now an almost opaline color.

"No, thank you, I don't really have time for that." Isabelle was halfway out the door when she realized her voice had lost its breathiness and she was almost shouting, making everyone in that too silent room stop for a moment and stare.

As she entered the foyer, she saw that standing at the front desk was the priest she had seen before; he was smoking a cigarette. He saw her storm from the sunroom and he looked at her with bemused confusion. He laughed a little to himself and then looked down. He was flipping through a newspaper and next to that was a large pile of letters that he was using to ash his cigarette on.

Isabelle was curious if those were the letters, she had sat next to on the ship ride here. When was that? Was it only yesterday?

She found herself staring at him as she started to slow her walk towards the hallway. She always hated priests. There were a few that would visit the almshouse when she was young, for 'counseling' reasons. She often found that the ones she was left alone with would ask her to sit on their laps, their hands would linger too long, their fingers and words feeling like the predatory talons and caws of large birds that fly in the night.

Isabelle did not know why she found this priest so interesting. He looked to be about 30 years old. He had a bone-weary posture and his eyes had a sardonic tiredness that made the fact of him having an air of holy grace seem almost impossible.

She was stopped dead in her tracks, looking at him like he was an animal in a cage. How long had he been here? She felt upon looking at him that he was somehow wound into this place. He was so seemingly at one with the desk he leaned over. He looked both comfortable and resigned to his fate, or was it his faith?

Yes, she hated priests.

She was staring at him, she knew she was, and in a way, she was thankful for the piercing cries of the baby hidden in her room. It distracted her, and only her. She looked up, craning her head towards the stairs, and almost darted up there before remembering where she was, and who she was. She was still staring, listening keenly, growing later to her meeting by seconds that now labored into minutes.

Could no one else hear this? Can no one hear him, Oscar?

"Love, love? Is something the matter?" She heard him saying this, though his accent was strange, his voice sounded thick with marbles.

"What?" Isabelle said. Remembering again where she was, where she was going. She had a meeting with Mister Hughes. Her hands came up again, wiping the hair away from her face, the imaginary cobwebs of her femininity that always threatened to tangle against her.

"I think you're meant to be someplace else," he said, again his words seeming almost indecipherable to her. She once again felt flush, and the crying seemed louder now than even a moment ago. She stood there, in the middle of the room, and instead of moving, she placed the palms of her hands against her ears. She closed her eyes. She felt the world tumble over her like waves. She felt the fingers and gentle tugging of the grundylow, and suddenly she was underwater.

She coughed imaginary water from her lungs and opened her eyes, to see that she was being tugged towards the hallway. The strong 'counseling' fingers of this holy man pulling her down the hallway and closer to Mister Hughes' office. He was whispering in her ear, words like secret messages that hardly made any sense. The words spoken in a frantic whisper, coming out so fast it was like Latin, she closed her eyes again, she smelled the ocean and thick incense of a church.

She heard the baby crying.

"You need to listen to me. Don't say more than you need to, be polite, and smile. Agree with him, it's easier. Tell me you understand me, you don't have much time."

She looked at him; unsure of what she heard was correct, what was just mixed up thoughts in her head. The baby, it was crying so loud now. Her eyes blurred and she tried to put her hands back up to her ears. He did not let her block the world away; he pulled her hands down again and tried to get her to look at him.

"Tell me you understand," he said again this time with urgency. She had somehow been walked down the hall and Isabelle could see the open door to what she assumed was Mister Hughes office.

"Just tell the good doctor, I mean *hotel manager* what he wants to hear. All right? And tomorrow and for the rest of the day, don't drink the tea." He said the last part in an almost silence. His lips moving with an almost absence of sound, "It will make you lose time, but trust me, it will always find you in the end."

She took the final few steps towards Mister Hughes' office alone after he gently pushed her towards the door.

When she took a quick final glance down the hallway, she was alone. Had the priest, the strange man in black been there at all with her, she was not sure. She walked into the office; a small man at a large desk was center stage.

"I'm sorry I'm late, I didn't get the note until it was already 7:30. My apologies." She tried to say the words with a casual but ladylike level of dignity.

"Nonsense, it's only 7:25, you're not late, you're actually early, and also, you said you got a note? That is strange; I did not send one. Nevertheless, you are here, let us get started."

Somewhere outside the room, she heard Daisy laughing. This sound was the only thing that could drown out the endless three minutes of Oscar's cries.

Chapter 13

She sat as politely as she could across from him, swishing her skirt in a demure yet becoming way before she took her seat. She folded her hands neatly and in doing so moved the outer pleats of her skirt that had the smeared stains of cinnamon blood, to a place that were hopefully less visible. She looked at him with a blank expectancy and made a face as if she were smiling.

She knew men were far more at ease when a woman, any woman was smiling at them.

"You're settling in." He said, not as a question as she was expecting, but as a definitive statement. She knew any other answer besides, yes would seem argumentative, and unstable. He did not ask her if she was settling in, but instead, told her. She remembered the words from the priest, real or imagined, and she knew what she had to say, she had to agree.

"Of course, it's quite a lovely . . ., she paused, and she wanted to say institution, or home. She knew she could just say the word, "building," but that would imply a coldness that she should not convey. She remembered her first weeks at the almshouse; she was so young and so newly orphaned. She understood after the first week of questions that no one really wanted answers they just wanted statements. They wanted smiles. They wanted agreeable girls, who were kind, and pretty . . . just not too pretty.

"It's quite a lovely hotel. I am lucky to be here. My husband made a good decision for me." She barely got the words out, when she heard Daisy's laughter again, it sounded like knives cutting meat that had been cooked too long. Her laughter scraped ceaselessly and sawed at something that never wanted to be cut or consumed.

"Well we are proud of it here. It has the best view of the ocean on the entire island. It is the rocks, they are very jagged and sharp, and so it makes the waves just spectacular, even in the best of weather. It makes the wind kick up too, so even on our hottest days the wind comes in as if it comes over ice fields. It is terrifying at first to people, but then they grow to love it. It is refreshing. Healing. You will see. You will feel it. It is why people come here, the air, the water; it helps our most exhausted guests finally get the rest the need." He said this, sounding so proud, so smug.

"Yes" Isabelle said. Realizing she didn't quite understand what her response should be. Should she tell him the water lived in her nightmares as a child. Should she tell him she could feel the grundylow and its spindling fingers wind their way into her throat when the wind blew? Instead, she thought of the advice given to her before any social gathering she had ever been forced into, be polite. Ask questions.

"How did you ever find such a remarkable place for the hotel Mister Hughes," Isabelle said this but was afraid inside that she was speaking too loudly; she knew she was trying to drown out a child's imaginary cry and Daisy's all too real laughter.

She could almost see Daisy leaning over the desk, sharing a cigarette with the priest; but when Daisy would let the ash fall from her cigarettes they would fall into a beautiful hatbox, the still warm edges of the smoldering ash making the baby hidden inside startle once again and cry out. Almost more awful to Isabelle, she could see the ashes turning the beautiful blue interior into mottled dirt and burned out book pages.

"It is funny you should ask; the land was my Father's. We originally thought it should be an artist retreat, it was my sister's idea really, as she was a poet . . ." His voice trailed off before it picked back up again like a siren's wail. " . . But the artists never came here. It was too violent for them. The waves and the wind too loud for them to think, that's what they would say." He paused waiting for Isabelle's response.

So, she smiled.

She laughed in a polite way, a way that said she heard him but that of course she could never really understand him. His intelligence was too great for her. It was that kind of laughter; the kind that felt like feathers against the insides of your arms. The kind of laughter that made you feel special and not derided.

"Well, it's a good thing you were smart enough to see what this place really was, not many men would see that. What it could be used for . . . How helpful it could be." She barely finished her words when he cut in.

"Yes, especially for women like you, who are so tired, what better place for you to come and rest? You have been through so much. It's almost normal that part of you would have broken away during all of it."

Broken away.

Isabelle wondered at that moment if it were true. Was there a part of her that had snapped off, gotten lost somewhere in her house over the past few months? She remembered the dark shadows that slept in the corners of her perhaps now former, home. She saw them now for what they were. Dark places where things go to hide and are never found.

Still the baby cried, and Daisy laughed. Isabelle turned her head slightly to try to hear beyond all of it, to the sound of the waves that were meant to heal her.

"You must be exhausted, so I won't keep you much longer," Mister Hughes said as he was already beginning to lean back in his chair and push away from the desk a couple inches, signaling that their meeting was almost finished.

"Actually . . .," Isabelle said, "I'm not that tired and seeing as it's just morning and the beginning of the day, I thought I should probably get acquainted with everything."

Mister Hughes stared at her and without much hesitation stated, "Sometimes we are more tired than we think we are. You may not even realize how tired you are. How could you?" He waited a few moments for a response, but Isabelle was not sure if that was really what was expected or wanted of her. Did they want her conversation, or did they want her agreement?

"Afterall Isabelle, I know what you have been through, probably even more than you know. I read the paperwork your Mother and Husband sent in."

"She's not my mother." Isabelle said this with little emotion and no hesitation.

"Excuse me?" He said.

"I'm sorry to sound rude but she isn't my mother, my mother died when I was a girl. Minnie, Mother Minnie is my husband's mother, not mine."

"Well dear, that sounds like a silly thing to be concerned with, you know your husband's mother is just as much of a mother to you as yours was; probably even more so." Mister Hughes began to flip through a stack of papers that seemed much larger than it should have. "Yes, I see here that your parents abandoned you when you were just a little girl, so of course, your mother-in-law is your mother now."

"They didn't abandon me, they died."

"Oh yes, of course, they died, but then none of your other family members wanted you That's right, I see that here. I also read in your files that after you were not taking care of yourself properly during your pregnancy and then gave birth to the stillborn child . . ."

"No, no he wasn't stillborn, he was alive, and then he died. He was alive though . . ."

"I think we're splitting hairs, it's really all the same thing in the long run. So, as I was saying, after the stillbirth, your mother and husband told us that you were actually playing around in the blood afterwards . . ." Mister Hughes sighed dramatically and seemed to wipe imaginary perspiration from his brow before he continued on, "That they found strange symbols written in his blood, hidden away in the bed you slept in." He almost looked as if he was stifling a gag as he finished saying the last part. He turned his eyes down, making himself busy with a constant shuffling of the papers.

"It wasn't strange symbols." Isabelle whispered. A deep shame burning inside her throat, it was shame that lived next to rage.

"Well, it says in your file that it was symbols, and there is no reason for your mother and husband to lie."

"There are plenty of reasons for them to lie." Isabelle said, challenging him with a momentary clarity of her stare, "And it was his initial. I wrote his initial in the blood. I knew his grave wouldn't have a name, and his name was Oscar."

"Well of course his grave wouldn't have a name; they don't name the stillborn babies . . ."

"He wasn't stillborn, he was alive, and now he's not. His name was Oscar." She was shouting by the end; she could feel herself becoming dizzy.

"See, you are becoming overtired, getting worked up for no reason, it happens. The first few days here are a transition. You will find your way, I promise you. You just need to rest." He reached his hand out to her and placed his large palm over her hand. It felt damp against her skin, and he squeezed her hand. "Now, I can have Daisy bring you some tea, and you could lie down until lunch, or we could get you a warm blanket and you could sit on the veranda and look at the water."

Isabelle remembered the whispers of warning from the priest; she could feel in her heart that she should say no. She should be strong; she should face the day, and feel that cold wind inside of her throat, the wind that feels like ice. She should lay awake while the baby cried. She should feel the three minutes, feel the grundylow tug at her skirts and feel the waves press over her.

She heard Daisy laugh again from somewhere outside the room. She thought about all of this and then decided she just could not do it; not now, not today.

"Yes, a tea would be lovely. Could you tell them to make it hot, and strong?" She looked up and with a knowingness in her eyes as she told Mister Hughes the exact things, he had expected her to say, the exact things he expected all of them to say.

"Of course, Ma'am, it will help, I promise you." He gave her a little wink when he finished talking.

"Thank you, Mister Hughes. She smiled and it felt like a tree that had long since fallen to rot, its roots did not lead anywhere, and neither did its branches. Things that once searched for water or sun have long since died.

All that was there was a dried-out husk where a woman used to be. She tried to widen her smile, and she heard branches snapping in the wind. She heard the baby crying again, and Daisy's laugh that seemed to swirl around her like a storm. She heard both, winding around each other . . . so far away that their voices blended into one white noise; a constant wail, a wind of hurt, blowing against her face.

A hidden door seemed to open behind Mister Hughes, and Daisy entered, she was so immediately part of the room. It was as if she arrived as the echoes of her laughter radiated through the building making her sound further and further away the closer she got.

"Tea Ma'am? I also brought you a blanket if you wanted to go outside. It is still early so I put it near the stove so it would be nice and warm, or you could just go on up to your room and still have the warm blanket. You could go outside later in the day . . . but here, just take this, you look a little shaken." Daisy handed her the tea, which looked to be an almost black green in color.

Isabelle did not know what was inside the cup, but she took it. Isabelle drank the whole thing, and immediately hated herself. The last thing Isabelle remembered clearly was her hand reaching out for the thick white cotton blanket, still warm from the stove, and then there was nothing at all, just images and misplaced puzzle pieces.

She thought she heard a baby crying and then a young woman's laughter.

She remembered a man dressed in black with a white collar, she remembered he was whispering something to her. She just could not remember what it was. She could almost feel his hand on her arm, guiding her somewhere.

She suddenly felt a cool breeze against her face, as someone placed her body down on an Adirondack chair, she looked out, and all she could see was the ocean, its tumultuous gray waves like the fingers of the grundylow, reaching out of the water and over the rocks. It was reaching for her; it was reaching for all of them.

Chapter 14

She woke hours later, the sun moving across the sky, making the day grow warmer around her, things grew sunny around her, but the sunlight never quite touched her skin. By the time she woke she had four blankets placed on her by, she can only assume, Daisy. They all seemed to hope for the curing nature of the air but did almost anything in their power to keep their patients, no, their guests from feeling it.

Her head felt heavy, the smoothed over rocks from the shoreline seemed to have found a new home inside of her. She turned her head slowly from side to side, noticing that she was not alone out there on that large veranda that spanned the entire front of the building. She had other sleeping companions, sitting vigil along with her, facing out to sea. She was the only one that seemed to be stirring though.

Her mouth was coated in a bitterness. It tasted not like the medicinal licorice that she was used to, no, this tasted different. It was earthier, damper. It tasted like clouds of white fungus, it tasted like the earth, not ocean sand, but something else, from the deepest parts of the forest. It tasted old, ancient and vile.

Her first instinct was to throw the blankets off her and dash madly almost blindly towards the water, to rinse her mouth. To replace that taste with a saltwater scream but she did not trust herself, not now, maybe if she was honest, not ever. She was clumsy, awkward, foolish, even when she was at her best . . . She knew the water, especially that water could, and would outthink her. It would know her insides; it would reach up and show them to her.

She stood up, and let the blankets fall to the wooden deck. She took three unsteady but large paces towards the railing of the porch; she leaned on it with all her weight as she stopped in order to get her bearings. Though her steps had felt loud and plodding to her own ears, she realized that she had not woken any of the other sleeping dolls.

That was when she realized, they were all women, at least out here they were. She had seen men at breakfast, hadn't she? That was when his face flashed in her head, the white collar. Yes, the priest, but was he a guest, an employee? He had been saying something to her before she met with Mister Hughes. It was a warning. She remembered that. Then she had to remind to herself that everyone was there for their own reasons, their own specific types of exhaustion.

She stared out at the water, willing herself finally to let go of the bannister, turn around and walk somewhere. It did not matter where, just somewhere.

"Ma'am?"

Isabelle turned around expecting to see Daisy but was met with a small freckled girl. She could not have been much more than fourteen and her hair was a bundle of wiry copper curls.

"Are you alright Ma'am? Is there anything I can do for you?" She spoke her words in a mild whisper as to not wake anyone else. Her voice was gilded over with an Irish accent, the kind that lilts instead of speaking in straight lines. She had a voice that would make anyone who hears it think that she was not a human at all, but a fairy changeling.

"Could you tell me what time it is?" Isabelle asked, trying to measure her own volume to match with the girl. "And I'm sorry, what was your name? I'm not sure if we have met yet?"

"I'm Nora, Ma'am, and no we haven't met yet. I can't quite say what the time is Ma'am, but from where the sun is, it looks to be somewhere between two and three. I'm afraid you were resting through lunch Ma'am, but that happens a lot here so it's not a bother if you want me to fetch a little plate of biscuits and some tea."

"What time is dinner Nora? I'm afraid I don't know what our schedule is supposed to be."

"Oh, that's fine Ma'am. Dinner is served at half past five in the dining room, not the room for breakfast. You won't be able to miss it; the doors will be open. You might want to have something before then though. I would be happy to get something warm for you."

"No, that's fine. Just a glass of water would be wonderful. I was thinking of going for a walk around the grounds. Get acquainted with the place." Isabelle paused only briefly before continuing, "I'd like to see where I am."

"Well that seems like a nice way to spend your afternoon Ma'am. I'll fetch water for you. Just make sure you don't take too long on your walk. Everyone meets for tea in the lobby around four. That way you can meet your new friends before dinner. Oh, and I hope you don't mind me saying, don't forget to change your dress Ma'am. That one you're wearing seems to have gotten a little dirty already, and it's sure to get worse traipsing around this place." With that, Nora turned abruptly and was gone in an instant. Her red tangle of wire curls almost left a trace in the air like a fire in the night.

She came back a few minutes later, with a small canteen of water that Isabelle drank from slowly at first, and then had to restrain herself from finishing the entire thing. She wrapped the strap around her body the way she had seen the soldiers do as they marched towards the train stations so many years ago as they headed south. She immediately felt as if her simple walk around the grounds were tantamount to her going off to war.

As she walked down the wide stairs to the grassy front lawn, she felt a bit unsteady on her feet, but with each step away from the hotel, her head seemed to clear. The fog began to lift and the cobwebs that slowed her thoughts seemed to part. She realized she had spent the past god knows how long living by means of clinging to sinews of her own memories. She had been tangled and weighed down by them for as long as she could remember. They were part of her, even long before Oscar was.

She took a deep breath, the cool salty air tasted good on her tongue like popcorn at a town fair. She could feel the air ride in off the ocean around her. She felt it already beginning to make the ends of her thick long hair begin to curl and puff up like a cat that got spooked by the wind.

There was no distinct path for her to take, other than the one leading down towards the dock, so she turned left and decided to circle the large property. She at first felt like she was running away. The strange desire to remain hidden always was so strong inside her. She realized as she walked, she clung close to the building. She was hugging its shadow and knew she would be unseen by anyone who may be looking out the windows. She was playing hide and seek by herself, the way she would when she was small after her parents died. She would hide for hours in the almshouse, in the large linen closet on the third floor. She knew no one would find her because no one was looking. There was a feeling of freedom in those hours that most people would find lonely.

She found solace.

When she made her way around to the back of the building, she became a little braver. She saw in the distance a small white gazebo by the rocky shoreline. To the left of that were the beginnings of a small trail leading into a copse of trees that seemed to grow straight out of the rocks. Their spindly trunks looked like fingers reaching out from between them, desperate for the sun. Her curiosity was piqued by the small path, the danger she felt at the thought of darting out from the safety of the building into the open space made her feel a mixture of queasiness and excitement that built up inside her.

She ran, childlike and free towards the little path. She could not remember running in the outdoors at all even as a child, this could have been the first time it had happened. Her legs felt heavy and awkward, unused. Her boots along the stone path sounded like a carriage with a warped wheel on a cobblestone street.

She made it across the wide expanse of lawn, thundering into the trees like she had won a race . . . She found herself surrounded on both sides by leaning birches, their branches curling almost over the path itself so at times it seemed like a tunnel. She would have to duck her head and shield her eyes to keep from being scratched.

The path led onwards in a twisting and turning pattern. She could tell she probably had not really gone far at all, maybe a few hundred feet, but the path kept winding back on itself like a sailor's knot. The ground became more and more uneven the closer she got to her imagined destination. She thought that it would eventually lead her to a small picnic place, or even a view of the deep open ocean. She imagined the poets and artists who used to stay at the hotel before it was taken over by weakness and disrepair of the mind. She imagined lovers sneaking though these woods with a bottle of wine, and both walking out with poetry born in their blood, waiting to be birthed onto the page.

She was lost in this fantasy and she barely realized that the trees had thinned, and the path had come to an end. She found herself in a small clearing, a twenty-foot radius where the sun shone in flat crisp light. She could not hear the water crashing into the shore with its almost deafening consistency. She could not hear the constant buzzing hum of the cicada that seemed to be swallowing her whole just moments before.

All there was was silence.

And the little graves. Some of them seemed quite new.

The graves of children, no, not children. Babies.

She remembered Daisy telling her there were no children allowed at the hotel.

She saw the freshly turned dirt marking the newest ones.

She felt herself grow flush; she was both frozen in the still air *and* soaked with sweat. She gagged a few times before getting sick just to the side of the trail directly behind where she stood, shocked. It was at this point that the cicada's hum was replaced by a sound of crying, the keening wail of a newborn and hidden somewhere beneath that, she heard laughter, and then a scream.

She did not realize that it was her making the noise until she began to feel her throat start to burn and feel as though it was being torn raw and ragged. She clamped her hands over her mouth, but she kept screaming, nonetheless.

Chapter 15

Isabelle had not realized that she had fallen to the ground until she felt someone had lifted her up and placed her back on her feet. Her cries were muffled now due to exhaustion but were still easily heard echoing through this place. They bounced off the stones and came back to her, hitting her like waves. Her sounds played off each little stone, each little mound of dirt, until it sounded like a symphony of wails.

Without turning around, she felt herself give in for a moment and relax her body against the still faceless person who heard her cries and came to her. Her breath began to even out. She closed her eyes, hoping the world would be different when she opened them, and it was.

When she opened her eyes, she was alone. The tiny graves of the small sleeping secrets still remained though. She turned around looking back down the path that she came from and saw no one there, the trees were still, and the air seemed close and filled with expectation. It seemed to shiver around her in wait.

She walked back to the hotel, realizing that her dress was filthy, and that she would have no choice but to change before dinner. She tried to look up towards the sky to get a feeling of the time, but she could not see through the canopy of the trees, they seemed to be holding her down, and holding her in. She tried to pick up speed but found her legs were trembling, and her spirit shaken, she was unsure of her footing.

When she finally made her way through the trees and found herself back on that large green lawn, she saw that the shadows of the hotel grew long and slender, reaching almost all the way to her. Where just a little while ago she found solace in the shadows, she now only felt unease, and chose instead to walk with a wide berth, making sure even her the edges of her skirt did not find themselves too close to the darkness.

As she approached the hotel she looked once towards the white gazebo, thinking to herself that would have been the safer location for her day's journey, it was then she saw him, staring at her.

The Priest.

He looked at her, with a sad sense of knowing. A look of condemned resignation on his face, he nodded at her politely and without waiting for a response from her, he turned his back to her and stared out at the sea.

She was able to enter to lobby with hardly a glance up in her direction. She was safely back in her pristine and spartan white room with the door closed before she was able really to breathe again. She peeled off her filthy skirt, the cinnamon claw marks from breakfast paled in comparison to the dirt and grass stains from her time in the graveyard. She felt the bile rise in her mouth when she thought of the dirt piles, thinking that it might be the same dirt . . . the little piles, the children that do not exist here at the hotel.

Isabelle kicked the skirt under her bed as if it were a wild thing, biting at her legs. In just her bustle and petticoat, she sat on the edge of her bed. The sheets made a crinkling noise as if their rigidity were being broken under her weight. It sounded like the icicles that would break off her house over the kitchen window, shattering onto the street after tumbling down the small embankment her home was perched atop.

Her home.

Her former home?

The house, yes, the house where she lived once and may live again; she was not sure.

She turned her head slowly back and forth, hearing the cricks in her neck that she got whenever she was tense begin to crackle. Every time her head would rotate to the right, she would catch a shy glimpse of herself in the small mirror that hung on the wall above the water basin. Her hair, which she had thought would have grown wild, still lay in an almost civilized manor in their dark heavy pleats. They looked like the curtain of a theatre, opening for a performance, and only revealing a blank stage, harsh lighting, and too many shadows crossing in all the wrong ways for no reason.

It was then that she realized that she had been out waking during the day, and in the sun. Yet, she had forgotten the sun hat. The thing that she never asked for, and only now she truly knew its worth. This was her most favorite unasked for piece of love.

She reached up and gingerly touched the red marks on her face that looked like burns, the top of her forehead, and across the bridge of her nose. She got up from the bed and took a few more steps towards the mirror to inspect herself. It was then she noticed the handprint. The color was a faint pink, the same color she turned when she was exposed to the sun, wind, or humiliation. This delicate handprint covering her mouth, the fingertips causing small print like bruises on her left cheek.

Her stifling her own screams created this scar, this momentary light shining on her darkness. She should have known better; her skin was the strange kind of pale that borders on the bluer hues in milk about to go bad. Its tenderness reacts to almost anything like meat that is almost raw on the inside and burned on the out. She started to pinch the rest of her face lightly to even out the red, it is better to be all red than just a little. Then she took her hairbrush, the stiff bristles felt sharp as brambles as she tried gently to brush them against her lips, making them swell just a little.

When she felt she was sufficiently reddened she put her pale powder over her whole face and looked at herself. She thought she looked like a tragic Italian clown from an opera she would never be smart enough or worldly enough to understand. Even though she felt garish and unseemly, she knew in her heart, that no one would look close enough at her ever to tell the difference.

Chapter 16

She arrived in the lobby and found that most of the 'guests' and staff were already milling around, awkwardly chatting with each other as if this was the world's saddest dinner party. The women, some of which were dressed in their finest, wore jewels and the strange woman who stared so intently at her cinnamon roll from breakfast even wore a fox wrap. It was the kind with small snarling face still attached, its little paws wrapping in an almost strangulation hold around the woman's neck. She stared accordingly at her own cup of tea in an almost hallucinatory ecstasy.

Welcome to teatime.

"Isabelle . . ." Mister Hughes' voice started out boisterous, but he dragged the last part of her name until it sounded almost predatory and sick like a cough that lingers for months long after you are well.

He strode over to her with such an overconfident and theatrical aplomb that Isabelle felt once again like the Italian clown with a frightening mouth and tear drop painted on their face; a constant screaming and laughing monster.

"Isabelle, you should meet one of our favorite guests." He grabbed her arm in the crook of her elbow and guided her towards the large woman with her vacant smile, and her snarling fox.

"Isabelle, this is Patricia, Patricia this is Isabelle. She is brand new here, and I trust you will make her feel most welcome during these early days. Isabelle . . ." again his voice dragged on too long at the end, as his hand lightened its grip on her, and he tried his best impersonation of tender.

"Patricia was one of our first guests here, isn't that right Patricia?" Mister Hughes did not wait for her to answer before he continued. How many summer seasons have you been with us, is it three? Yes, it is three now, isn't that right?"

"Oh yes, yes three years. My Harold sent me here three summers ago and he just loved it so much." She paused awkwardly as if for a moment she shut down completely. Her face looked as though a book had shut and then was immediately reopened but the reader had lost their place. "I mean we, *we* loved it so much . . . me being here. I went home so rested, so happy." Her voice was slow, like cold molasses seeping out of a pitcher on a morning when all you long for is comfort or warmth. Instead you find nothing but confusion and, in the end, disappointment. Her voice fought against the strong tides of the ocean and came to Isabelle in this room bogged down in seaweed and shipwrecks.

Patricia's doughy and uncooked hand raised the teacup to her mouth; it gave off a faint tremor before it met her lips.

"Oh, how rude of me, Isabelle you have no tea." Mister Hughes said this loudly to cover the sounds of the precarious rattle of teacup against saucer as Patricia tried to place it there in a way that made them all seem "normal."

She heard the memory again ringing in her head, "don't drink the tea" it drowned out the three minutes of Oscar's crying just for a moment. Isabelle scanned the room, noticing that all the women had teacups, warbling in shaking hands. The men, of which there was more than she thought, but not as many, were not drinking the tea. Instead, they all had what appeared to be whiskey or brandy in clear dignified glasses.

112

The men were grouped together, they laughed, and they sounded alive. There was energy radiating off them like waves, it made her uneasy. She was scared to be there, with her reactions being so slow. The male laughter continued in bursts like gunfire. It sounded angry, and frustrated.

From the women, there were mainly confused murmurs. All having pretend conversations with each other, they had placid smiles on their faces as they all stared out into nothing. They moved their mouths as if they were background actors in a play. It was pretend conversations. Isabelle could almost imagine a director calling out to all the women in this hideous antechamber, "If you smile and move your mouths it won't matter that you are not saying anything."

"Mister Hughes, even though I have only been here a couple days, I find that I am quite missing home. Before dinner my husband and I always had a little brandy or when we were feeling chilled a bit of whiskey. Could I have that instead?" Isabelle said, moving her mouth, and not really saying anything at all.

Mister Hughes pinched her under her arm and pulled her about two feet away from the porcine face of Patricia. "Mrs. Baker, I'm sorry but we believe in temperance here, and it is always unseemly to see a lady drinking during the day. But . . . we can make an exception this once and get you some sherry if that would make you feel . . . more at home."

"Yes, that would be nice, thank you," Isabelle said, with a cloying demure sincerity that she would on occasion have to use on Henry when she had angered him unknowingly. Mister Hughes turned his back to her and waved one of his arms frantically to get someone's attention; someone on a different tier in the hierarchy that he was, a woman perhaps, to fetch the sherry.

"Hawthorne," a voice interrupted and at first Isabelle was entirely confused as to what this person was saying, she did not understand until she saw Mister Hughes turn towards the voice. His voice.

113

"Oh, Father, yes, can I help you with something?" Mister Hughes said in an almost startled embarrassment.

"Jesus, Hawthorne, how many times do I have to say it, you can just call me Francis when I'm here. We're not in a church." He gave off a sad and almost sheepish laugh. His hand went almost instinctively to his white collar, tugging ever so slightly away from his skin as if when he used the word Jesus it had made it tighten around him like a wire trap meant for rabbits. It reminded Isabelle of the way that unhappily married women would almost always wind their wedding rings around their fingers in an uncontrolled tick. It was an act that lived somewhere between mania and prayer.

"I just thought I should bring our new guest a drink." His eyes left Mister Hughes' face and traveled to Isabelle. Again, she saw that knowing sadness in them, and it made her feel for the first time in her life, seen.

"I saw you outside walking, and the wind can often chill the ladies when they aren't used to it. I brought you a little of my favorite." With that, he handed her a clear, dignified, and masculine glass, a smoky brown liquid filled the bottom two inches of it. This was not a polite woman's sherry. This she thought, was the whiskey she had wanted to feel on her tongue since she arrived.

"Thank you, Father," she said, suddenly blushing underneath her pale face powder; she could feel the hand shaped bruise underneath her painted facade begin to throb.

"Like I told Hawthorne, you should call me Francis. We're all friends here. Well, most of us." He continued to look at her, staring straight into her eyes with a dare. It was unsettling. The look on his face was not so much that he was looking at her but looking inside of her, seeing it all. The ugly parts of her, the sad pieces of decay that grow inside her, the things she would keep tucked away in a hatbox, next to a baby all things grown still and blue . . . She could still hear him talking but couldn't quite make out what he was saying.

"I'm sorry, could you repeat that?" She whispered, her eyes for some reason filling with tears. Without letting Francis answer her, Mister Hughes cut in instead, she had almost forgotten he was standing there with them; the world had grown dark around the edges until she could hardly see anything. It was strange thing that happened on an off to her since she was small and was first sent to the almshouse.

"This is Mrs. Baker. Her husband and mother thought she deserved a nice peaceful stay with us for the summer, isn't that right Mrs. Baker?"

"She's not my mother; she is my husband's mother. And yes, yes, they thought I was tired." Isabelle said, as if she was disclosing something awful. They also thought I had done something unseemly with blood." She paused, "I assure you that part was a misunderstanding.

"Well, that's strange because you don't seem tired to me, and if we're honest I think a lot of us have probably done some unseemly things with blood." Francis said this, with a hint of kindness; the way a grown up would try to get a child to smile after they had just dropped their favorite toy in the street and it came back filthy with mud and lost dreams.

"Sometimes you're more tired than you think you are." She said this, and finally looked at him in the face, her eyes telling him as much as she could without words, as much as she was willing to tell a stranger. That she was here against her will, that she was there as punishment for so many things; for having Oscar when he was too small and too sick to survive, for not understanding how it was that she was supposed to grieve, and for the worst part of all, for her body being shattered and breaking inside her. The birth leaving her womb nothing more than a tattered old book of gruesome tales better left untold, and no baby, no son, no heir.

No future.

Francis nodded silently, and Isabelle took the silence as an invitation to finally sip the drink that she hoped would silence those keening baby cries long enough for her to get through dinner.

"I should go make sure the name cards are placed correctly for dinner tonight. Mrs. Baker I will have you dining with Patricia tonight. You two have so much in common. Father, you will be at my table as usual, with Agnes." With that, Mister Hughes left, without so much as a goodbye to Isabelle, and with an overly masculine clap on the back towards Francis.

They waited a few moments until he was out of earshot before either of them exhaled. Their shoulders collectively dropped, and a sense of ease washed over them.

"Thank you for this." Isabelle said as she gestured with the glass. "I thought I would be stuck with the tea all night, or sherry. I've never even had sherry." She laughed a little and found herself suddenly unafraid that she would seem low class or uncouth. Which were things she lived her life in constant fear of with Henry. "My name is Isabelle. Please don't call me Mrs. Baker, that's my mother, mother-in law, and she is . . . awful. Just an awful sort of woman." She laughed again, perhaps the whiskey was hitting her a little harder than she expected. Before she could stop herself, she continued, "I cannot believe his name is Hawthorne, Hawthorne Hughes. It is almost laughably proper." She paused again and felt the heat of the liquor rising to her face.

Francis smiled and kept his voice low while saying, "He likes to pretend he lives up to the name, but he doesn't." He looked around the room quickly before reaching into the interior pocket of his black jacket. He pulled out a small flask and poured a little more into Isabelle's glass. He wound the cap back on the flask with one hand and made a shushing motion with his other. "You won't tell tales about me will ya' Isabelle?"

His smile alternated almost imperceptibly between heartbroken and mischievous. He looked to be a little younger than Isabelle was,
116

but with a lean and haunted look that it felt as though you were in the presence of something ancient when you looked at him.

"Don't worry, I won't say a word," she said, tying to sound lighthearted. She did not want to keep talking but she did. "What do you think he meant that Patricia and I would have a lot in common?"

"Oh, I don't know, she's been here a few years now for the summers. She has two daughters at home; she slowly poisons them throughout the winter, arsenic in small doses until they get almost too sick. Her husband doesn't want to make a fuss, so he sends her here in the spring until autumn to let the girls get well."

Francis looks away from Isabelle and takes a long slow sip form his glass before he says, "You don't strike me as the poisoning type though Isabelle. And you remember what I said to you this morning, don't you?" He whispered this, his eyes once again darting through the room with an edge of paranoia.

Isabelle began to wonder why it was that Father Francis was here at all. She remembered something form the morning, but she knew she was not exactly sure what it was, but rather than upset him she looked at him and smiled in her most comforting way and said. "Of course, I do." Before her smile could fade from her face, Daisy entered the room, rang a brass bell four times and the small group dispersed into the dining room.

Chapter 17

Isabelle was not sure what she had expected from the dining room.

She half thought that it would be filled with one large and uncomfortable table that they would all sit at, as if they were all the mad descendants from a royal family. But much like the breakfast set up; there were a series of tables set up throughout the room so at first glance it looked like a public house.

Isabelle sat at a small table for two with Patricia and realized almost right away that she might as well have been eating alone. Her companion spent most of the time, staring in absolute adoration at every bite of food she almost shoveled into her mouth. She would chew each bite twenty-three times which Isabell realized because she would always whisper the words "twenty-three for you and me," after each bite. She would then tap the table three times and start again. It was a ritual that seemed to both give her companion complete joy, but also exhaustion. The main course was especially grueling. The meat was unidentifiable, maybe pork? In the end it was tough and gamey. Isabelle could see that some of the time Patricia would be swallowing food that was not yet ready to swallow. She would almost choke it down, take a sip of tea, say her magic words, tap the table and start again.

Isabelle tried a few times to look over at Francis, eager with adolescent need to grab his attention; she wanted to share a laugh at this poor woman's expense. In her heart, Isabelle knew she was cold and unfeeling. Yet every time she looked over at his table, he was staring down at his plate; he looked to be eating mainly bread. She did see, not that she was trying to keep track of course, that he received three more additional refills of whiskey. They were all brought to him by Daisy, who would fill the glass four fingers worth, giggle and then curtsey. He never looked up, he never noticed Daisy, or even Isabelle at all.

Tea was served with desert and Isabelle who was feeling a little tired and giddy from the whiskey, drank the entire cup. She missed her laudanum. She hated herself for thinking it. She hated her longing for the great alone that it brought her, the days she would spend in the gloaming between the nothing and life.

As she saw people beginning to get up and leave, she instinctively looked for Francis, but it seemed like he was already gone. "What happens now?" Isabelle asked Patricia, who had finally come out of her counting and tapping reverie.

"Oh, it's free time for the next few hours really. Some people play cards, others get a book from the library and read outside, it is early in the season for that though, the nights are still cold. You can always bring a book to your room. It is usually quiet. If you stay down here, Daisy comes around with tea before bed, or that little one, Nora, if she's around will bring it to your room if you ask. It's just your first night; no one would think you were rude if you just went upstairs to rest."

They moved from the dining room to the lobby again, there were a few men sitting off to one corner of the room, already dealing cards. There was one older woman rocking in a rocking chair, her eyes were closed. Instead of the rocking being a soothing thing of comfort, it was fast, it seemed angry and only growing angrier with each repetitive movement.

There was another young woman, probably not older than sixteen or seventeen, playing quietly on the piano. Isabelle recognized

120

her as the young woman who sat next to Francis at dinner. The Piano was dreadfully out of tune and it made it all more heartbreaking a scene. Isabelle turned to ask Patricia where the library was but saw that she had already walked away, a cup of tea on a saucer balanced in one hand, and her long layers of skirts in the other.

These people, these fellow kings and queens of this summer hotel, they didn't seem ill, not in the way she feared they might. Instead, they just seemed sad, like toys discarded in an old steamer trunk for too long, and by the time you go back to find them they had grown old, dusty, and pieces were missing. The pieces that made you love them once are now trapped at the bottom of the box, with missing buttons and the faint whispers of the good memories from childhood.

There were very few of those shadow memories that Isabelle could remember. There were plenty of broken toys though, and tonight it seemed like all the broken pieces of her life were here living in an old house by the sea. She could see it clearly now. They had all somehow crawled from the box and arrived here.

Without knowing what time it was, Isabelle suddenly felt herself growing both anxious and tired. Those strange feelings you get when you suddenly felt exposed, standing in a room and not doing anything except try to be invisible. She wanted more than anything to find the library, but the thought of walking up to one of these strangers, one of these broken things and asking them, she could hardly bear it.

The music played on coming from the hunched over figure at the piano, the off-tune notes, made what should have been a lighthearted tune sound more like someone begging for help as they sunk under water.

The grundylow.

She could almost feel it now, tugging at her skirt and then her legs. Its fingers wrapping around her ankle, creeping up her calf, and almost to her knee . . . She knew she had to move, to find her way out of the imaginary creature's grasp.

She had made it to the stairs when she heard Nora's lilting voice, it seemed thick with a day's worth of exhaustion. "I'll bring a cup of tea to your room in few minutes Ma'am."

"Yes, yes thank you," Isabelle said before turning and walking up the stairs. She wondered if she would be the only one on the third floor for much longer, she had heard people saying it was 'early in the season' but she was not exactly sure what that meant. She wondered if soon all the rooms would be filled with women and men who cried during the night.

As she walked up the stairs, she felt the day envelope her, her shoulders sagged underneath the weight of this seemingly endless day as it dragged her through to the night almost against her will. She was alone in her room for just a few minutes when she heard the tentative knock on her door. It was three successive knocks that seemed to roll in a cadence, and she knew it was Nora with the tea.

When she opened the door, she saw the tea was placed on the floor, on a small silver tray that was in desperate need of polish. She saw the red tangle of Nora's curls bounce as she ran down the stairs without looking back at all. Isabelle bent to pick up the tray, and that is when she saw that next to the teacup was a small shell of a moon snail. She picked it up, letting her fingers work themselves over the delicate winding texture of it. For some reason, it gave her chills. She put the tray down and reached under the bed for the hatbox, she lifted the lid slowly and delicately as if not to wake the imagined child asleep inside. She lifted the hat, placed the shell underneath, and whispered the name Oscar, before placing the hat back down over it. She closed the lid and slid the box under the bed.

She drank her tea as she took off her heavy dinner dress, and before she could finish it, she realized she was exhausted. She laid her face against the pillow, her face powder immediately leaving a scar, soiling the crisp white perfection of the linens like rusted water on snow. It was her last thought of the day, before everything inside her shut off.

She did not wake to the sounds of the phantom children as they howled and cried through the night, but whether or not it happened, she knew she would never know.

Chapter 18

She woke the next morning, before dawn. The dark navy of the sky was just starting to brighten and blush in the distant horizon over the water. Her body felt once again as if she had not moved at all during the night, each stretch of her joints was a chore. Her hands had been balled into tight fists as she slept. As she uncurled her fingers, it was with an aching relief. The abrupt change of this sensation for some reason made her want to pull her fingers back into their fists again. She had to resist that urge and decided to rub her hands together instead; she felt them slowly come back to life.

She noticed the nearly empty teacup on the table near her bed; she had the sudden urge to throw the cup against the wall, to hear it shatter as the pieces fell to the floor like rain. She wanted to hear noise; the deafening silence seemed unnatural. She had an unnerving fear that she was alone in this summer hotel. She thought if she walked downstairs, she would find everything coated with dust and the walls whispering stories and telling secrets.

She knew it was too early for breakfast but thought perhaps there might be people up and about downstairs already. She dressed quickly. She rinsed her face in the basin of last night's water, inspecting herself closely in the mirror for any trace of the red marks she had given herself yesterday. She appeared at first glance to be normal. She thought for a moment that it did look like her pupils were unnaturally dilated, causing her eyes to look almost a solid black, like

125

the images of demons from the illustrated bible she was given when she entered the almshouse. She peered deep into her own eyes, until she did not recognize them as her own.

She let out a small gasping laugh, which made her realize that she had been holding her breath. She was imagining things; she was sure of that. It was due to the room being dark, which is all it was. It was all it could be. She could feel her paranoia burn up her back like a heat rash, it moved its way up until it reached her neck and made the base of her skull almost ache with fear.

Isabelle thought that she should ask Father Francis about the demon eyes, she wondered if he believed in demons, and if they did exist, how factual those illustrations were in that book of hers.

She found herself alone in the lobby, but in the distance, she could hear a bustling behind a set of swinging doors behind the front desk. Knowing she was not alone in this oversized dollhouse gave her a sense of comfort. She walked through the room, inspecting the furniture, the multitudes of paintings of lighthouses that hung in all shapes and sizes on one wall. It took her a moment to realize that they were all the same lighthouse, each one just a little different. Some were slightly askew, others seemed almost unrecognizable, just a large column of the right colors.

Were these remnants of the hotel's days as an artist retreat, or the workings of a mind that had grown obsessed and strange?

"What are you doing down here?" A high pitched voiced that sounded almost overripe with forced girlishness forced Isabelle to turn around, feeling both chastened and annoyed. She saw it was the girl from last night who played the piano. "No one is ever down here this early, this is when I practice." She continued talking as she almost stomped over to the piano, lifting the lid over the keys with an angry flip.

"I won't bother you, don't worry." Isabelle said.

"Well just having you here will be a distraction, see, I am already distracted, I should be playing but I'm not." As she said this, she moved her heavy bustled skirt and sat on the piano bench in a huff. Seeing her up close, Isabelle was right in her guess from last night, she could not be more than sixteen. She acted like a petulant child with her over dramatic and exasperated sigh. "You should go now."

"Well you didn't have any problem playing last night when everyone was here. I'd love to hear you play again . . ." Isabelle was cut off by the young girl slamming both her fists against the keys repeatedly in a tantrum.

"That was not practice last night that was performing; performing is what I do for all of you. Practice is what I do for me." She turned around and glared at Isabelle, her fists still pounding on the keys, the low notes, then the high ones, then the low and then the high.

These were not the sounds that Isabelle had longed to hear this morning. Even though she found the silence too overwhelming.

Suddenly the swinging doors from behind the desk opened and Daisy stormed out, her small features bunched into the center like a knot. "Agnes! Enough! Do not make me tell Mister Hughes how you are behaving. You will lose your piano privileges the way you did last summer, do you remember how unhappy you were then?"

"But Petal, you know how I need to concentrate to practice" Agnes whined.

"Ma'am, if you would like, I'm opening the breakfast room now and you are welcome to sit in there, you could get any table you like seeing you're the first one here. Or you are welcome to stay here." Daisy aimed the last words directly at Agnes who had masked her face in an aloof and contradictory manor.

"I think I will find a nice spot, thank you Daisy," Isabelle said and followed her into the sunroom. "She called you Petal?" Isabelle smirked a little, momentarily feeling as if they were just two friends gossiping about a girl they found tedious.

"Ugh, she knows I hate it, and I've corrected her countless times, but she heard Mister Hughes call me that and now she won't let it go. She is a gruesome little thing; you should stay clear of her. She loves to taunt people. She can get under your skin and in your head." Daisy began to set the silver and napkins on the tables, and Isabelle took a two-person table near the corner by the window. Giving her a view of everyone when they walked in and keeping her back snugly up against the wall.

The stiffness she felt upon waking up had not worked its way out of her body yet, and she thought that she should go walking again after breakfast but remembered the little graveyard from yesterday and began to think better of it. It was not so much the small stones that bothered her, but the freshness of the dirt that made her realize how terrible a place it was.

The room began to fill, as people petered in, most seemed like shambling sluggish creatures. Somnambulists with their eyes still open. Isabelle knew who she was waiting for, was hoping for. She only hoped that Patricia would not come in first and take the seat that was empty across from her.

Isabelle began to fidget with her hands, winding them and pulling at her own fingers. She started to peel her fingernails, pulling them off in jagged long pulls that sometimes went all the way down to the quick. It was a terrible habit, and one she tried her hardest over her life to break, but never seemed to manage it. There was always this waiting on the edge of tragedy that would cause the habit to start up again. She looked down in front of her and saw the small pile of fingernails she had accumulated; some had small bits of skin and blood on them. With her nails peeled down so short, she often thought her hands resembled a child's. Suddenly embarrassed she swept the fingernails underneath her water glass and out of her own eye shot.

When she looked up, she saw that he had entered, Francis, Father Francis. He was sitting one table over from her, in a chair that strangely faced her directly. They were sitting together almost, but apart.

He smiled. She noticed his lips curled unevenly across his teeth and he had a small scar running from his upper lip to his nose. It was the kind of scar that had long since shed itself from a puckered red welt and aged into a thick white line. She knew it was an old scar, a childhood trauma, scratched onto his face. A daily reminder of something that was probably better if it was forgotten.

"Good morning Isabelle."

"Good morning Francis."

"I trust you slept well last night, probably no dreams you can remember right?" He was talking to her, but staring straight ahead, not making eye contact.

She was curious why he would end such a polite question with something so strange, but she answered truthfully as if it were an unwritten law, that you cannot lie to a Priest.

"No, no dreams last night." She said with a touch of pride creeping into her voice. She could feel the courage being born under her skin when she was not beaten through the night with dreams and hallucinations.

"That must be very refreshing for you." He turned now and stared at her, unblinking for a little longer than what made her feel comfortable. She could not tell if he was sincere or challenging. She tried to keep the eye contact going for as long as she could but found that she could not. She had to turn away. Isabelle tried to reach for her glass of water but snatched her hand away from it as if it had scalded her. She remembered the ripped fingernails underneath it and thought better of exposing the broken bits of herself right now.

"Are you saving that seat across from you for your friend?" He asked in a teasing way, as if he could hear her thoughts and agony of her forced dinner with the porcine Patricia last night.

"I wouldn't really call her my friend, so no . . . I was about to ask you the same question," almost uncertain of how to proceed in this conversation or even her thoughts, she paused, "Will you be dining with Mister Hughes this morning; you seem very close?"

"Oh no, he doesn't eat with us commoners in the morning." He laughed, and his hand came up towards his face, hiding his scar and the way it tuned a normal smile or laugh into a biting sneer that he didn't want shown." With his hand still partially covering his face he continued, "We're not friends; I couldn't be friends with a man like him." Francis lowered his hand again once his face was not moving.

"Well, you seem to have a different sort of relationship to him than the other *guests* do." It was hard for Isabelle not to refer to them as patients, or worse, inmates.

"Oh, yes, I hear his confession every day, and because I do that, I am allowed certain privileges. On a good day I can almost imagine I'm free." His upper lip trembled a little as he said the last part, and she saw his hand shaking as it instinctively went up towards his face.

Isabelle looked at him, and for the first time she really saw him for what he was, another broken toy in a discarded box. They were the same probably, deep down inside. The kind of broken things that probably could have been fixed if anyone had ever bothered to notice there were small cracks forming all along.

"Why are you here?" She whispered.

"I can't hear you if you are going to whisper, you are too far away," he said, and she could hear the passive almost invitation for them to sit closer to each other in his voice.

"Well then maybe you should sit here across form me, then I won't have to whisper, and you won't have to shout." Isabelle was very suddenly annoyed at the made-up rules that she had been shackled to her whole life. All the politeness begins to eat away at someone from the inside. A lifetime of smiles and lies and she is only just realizing that until this morning she has never had a conversation with someone who listened to her and did not just simply wait to speak.

She was afraid that one day she would open her mouth to thank or forgive someone who did not deserve it, and all that would come out from her insides would be thick black blood. Years of holding in truth would suddenly come out of her like a flood.

Francis got up without a word and walked to her table, the six feet of distance that had seemed like a great cavern suddenly down to less than two feet. Only a small table and too much cutlery and napkins separated them.

"Now what was that you were whispering so politely at me before?" Again, the half-smile and the instinctive hand going up to hide it.

"Why are you here?" She said as she leaned over the table with a posture as if they were both conspiring against the world. She realized she was still whispering, but this time it had a sense of camaraderie. Something she had not felt in so many years. She remembered feeling close with some of the girls in the almshouse, they would whisper to each other at night when all the lights were out, silly games where they would tell each other their favorite things about other person. Sometimes even now she closes her eyes and can hear her friend Molly whispering to her in the night, "You have the prettiest mouth I have ever seen." Isabelle had never in her life felt as close to someone as she did to Molly, and she had never felt more loved than she did when she heard those words.

"They thought it was best I come here, I was here last summer and well they thought it helped . . . I'm not sure it did though, not

131

really." He said, also whispering, but his had a sense of shame to it, a sense of confessional behavior. She did not know how to respond, what prayers to give him for absolution.

"Who are they?" She said, not knowing if he meant family, or . . .

"The Bishop, and the church that I am in charge of, well was in charge of, they thought I should step away, take a break." His eyes darted around the room, and though Isabelle felt he was telling the truth, she also felt that he was leaving things out.

"But why, what did you do?" She asked, but even then, she was afraid to know the answer. She remembered the priests that would visit the almshouse, she remembered their lingering hands, their fingers that would wind under the collar of her shirt and tickle her on the back of her neck.

"I stopped believing in God, and worse than that, I stopped faking it. Once it was gone, that faith, I didn't know how to get it back. Then I didn't know if it was ever there to begin with. That love, that faith. I woke up one morning and realized that even if there was a God, he wasn't here; he wasn't inside me. I've never heard him talking to me." He laughed a little, "I may have heard other voices, but I haven't heard his."

That is when she noticed it again, the lip quiver, and the shaking hands. He picked up her glass of water and took a sip. If he saw her fingernails under there, he was kind enough not to mention them. He kept the water glass in his hands and looked out the window. This gave Isabelle enough time to sweep the nails onto the floor.

He put the glass down, reached inside his jacket, and pulled out the flask. He took a quick sip of the whiskey it held, and almost immediately, his hands stopped shaking.

"I don't know how many Hail Mary's to give you for your sins," she said, her voice was joking but soft.

132

"Oh, don't worry about it. My Ma has been saying them for years, I think now they just bounce right off of me." He smiled when he mentioned her, his mother, and this time when he smiled, he didn't hide that scar above his lip.

She was about to ask about his family when Nora and her bouncing mop of red wiry doll hair came to their table with their breakfast trays. She smiled at both, letting her vibrant green eyes linger for several moments longer on Francis. If it was noticed by him on some level, he ignored it.

"And what about you Isabelle, why are you here? Did you not wash the dishes properly? Did your husband find you napping during the day?" He tried to lighten a conversation that he probably knew would never turn out light.

She took a deep breath, and instead of letting it out, she held onto it, until a hint of a dark night and creeping stars started to encroach on the edges of her vision. She finally exhaled and then started, "I had a baby, and he died. He lived for just a few minutes, I wasn't allowed to hold him, or even see him."

"I'm sorry, Isabelle I shouldn't have . . ."

"No, it's fine, you should have asked, its fine. He died and I was not the right kind of sad. I am still not sure what kind of sad I was supposed to be, somedays they thought I was too sad, then not sad enough. Then Henry, my husband realized I would never be able to have children, and he felt just bad enough for me that he didn't want to send me to an institution the way his mother wanted him to, so this was the compromise. Also, apparently, I am very tired, more tired than I think I am." Isabelle said this all very plainly, very matter of fact. She left out the laudanum, the phantom child's cries from her hatbox; she left out the shadows that become real at night, the ones with hands. She left out the creeping grundylow and the monster's fingers that reach inside her.

"Isabelle, Isabelle . . ." She heard his voice, it seemed to come from far away, and she hadn't realized that her eyes were pinched shut until she opened them, and the room seemed overly bright. The light hitting her eyes, pupils still dilated and open. If felt as if she was staring at the sun.

"I'm sorry" she said, always apologizing first and then trying to figure out what she did wrong this time, second.

"You ever need to apologize to me; I just didn't really know where you went there for a little while . . ."

She looked at Francis, and looked down at his breakfast plate, which was mostly empty. Hers remained untouched. She wanted to ask how long her eyes had been closed, how long she had "been away," but she was afraid to know. She instead reached for a bite of her now cold eggs and toast. The bread was chewy, and bland. Without thinking anything of it, her hand instinctively reached for the teacup and she drank. It was not until she put it down that she looked at Francis' cup and saw that it was still full.

"It might good if after breakfast you went to your room to rest, maybe don't go out walking today. Originally, I thought about sneaking into the kitchen and stealing the leftover cinnamon rolls from yesterday and asking you for a picnic, but I think that should wait until tomorrow." He finished his sentence and then looked at the teacup with accusation in his eyes.

"What's in the tea? Do you know?" She whispered again. She knew she wanted an answer, but just one specifically. She wanted to hear that it was laudanum, the name of her very closest friend over the past many months.

"I'm not sure what it is. I know it keeps you quiet. Really just the women, but sometimes the men, I think they sneak whatever it is into the booze sometimes, or the food. It seems mainly for the women though."

"Do they know? The women that have been here every summer, do they know?" Isabelle realized after she said this that even though she 'knew' she couldn't be sure she would not just go along with it, anyway, still drink the tea. Isn't it better after all at the end of the day to feel nothing, rather than feel too many things?

"I'm not sure they care really; they are probably grateful for it. You don't need to be. I see you; you don't need to live an imagined life you can . . ."

She realized then that his voice was getting further and further away, getting slower. She knew when he talked to her he was talking to that girl inside her, the one who heard, "You have the prettiest mouth I have ever seen," the one who's thoughts are overcome by the sounds of a baby who screams forever, for three minutes that stretches all the way through time and comes back to her. He is talking to her, the woman who runs from the darkest shadows once she realizes they have hands that can touch you . . .

Francis is talking to her and the world fades away. She thinks of his voice and tries to hold onto that like a person with a life vest who has gone overboard. She hears his voice; his accent sounds to her the way that hands that are chapped from doing too much laundry feel when you rub them against each other. She wants to tell him that she knows him too, that she heard love in his voice when he said *Ma*, and she also heard the screaming silence when he didn't say the word father. She shudders inside because she called him Father in her head. She looks up; she sees the scar on his face, the white rope that runs up from his lip. She can almost feel a broken glass being smashed into his face when he was a boy. She thinks all of this, she feels in inside of her. She tries to make her mouth move, and the only thing that comes out is the blood of the lies she has told to herself over the course of her whole life.

She pinches her eyes closed.

A baby cries for three minutes.

135

She sees the lid to the hatbox slowly closing as his cries, which had grown weaker muffle completely.

She screams

The blood comes from her mouth.

The lies.

She screams again, this time even louder.

She sits up in her bed . . . Still wearing the dress she wore to breakfast. The sky is almost the same color as it was when she woke up. For a moment, she thinks it is all a dream, a morning that never happened.

A mourning that never happened.

Then she looks outside. The sun paints the sky in orange hues as fog and mist creep in. The fog does not dance over the ocean the way it does in the morning. She feels the gloaming around her. It comes in heavy and weighs on her like wet wool. She hears the call of sea birds and they sound like Oscar. She thinks for a moment that she is their mother. She can almost feel the wings and feathers rip through the skin on her back and she becomes them, and they are she.

She breaths in and out, blocking everything else out.

It is silent. She is laying in her bed. The gulls are silent; the ghost child screaming in the box under her bed is silent. She whispers a polite thank you to the air around her; she can almost taste the blood-tinged bile of her life rise inside of her like a red tide.

Chapter 19

A tentative knock at the door brings her back to reality. She instinctively goes to check her reflection in the mirror before opening the door. She notices that the room has grown dark and strange around her. The light has shifted and what little is left only whispers through the window like a secret.

She opens the door, and in the moments before she does it, she realizes she wants it to be Francis. She knows she should not want that, she can't want that. She does not want to be the silly kind of woman who falls in love with anyone who gives her the slightest attention. She opens the door a few inches and sees that it is Daisy, holding a tray.

"Ma'am, we thought we should bring up a tray for you after your spell this morning. Mister Hughes thought it best if you stayed in tonight. He said you probably caught a chill when you came over on the boat and it's just catching up to you now. You should be careful, especially in a hotel on an island, if one person gets sick it spreads like fire."

Isabelle listened to all of it intently, trying to rack her brain for any memory of breakfast this morning. She remembered Francis, his confession. She knows his voice faded from her and bounced around the insides of her head, another pebble in the well.

137

"Forgive me Daisy, I'm a little confused about what happened this morning."

"Well, you were eating with the Father, and he said it looked like you were confused, and then before he knew it you just stopped working, like a wind-up toy that needed winding. Then he said you fainted, he tried to catch you, but he ended up just knocking most of the things off the table." Daisy said all of this as she walked into the room and placed the dinner tray on the table by her bed. "When you're done with this you can just put the tray in the hall and I will come for it later, no sense in you going all the way downstairs." As she was about to leave, she suddenly turned to Isabelle. "Oh, and the Father wanted me to give you this, he thought it would help pass the time." Daisy handed a book to Isabelle. "He said he thought you would appreciate it."

Isabelle ran her hands over the cover, it was well worn, and the corners were blunted and starting to split. The textured brown cover felt almost like leather, and the gold words of the title almost completely worn away. She opened to the title page, it was stained with water damage and the paper felt brittle, and precious.

"Wuthering Heights," Isabelle said aloud.

"Excuse me Ma'am?" Daisy said.

"The book, it's Wuthering Heights, it's my favorite." Isabelle whispered that last part, as she let her fingers trace over the paper like it was a holy relic.

"Well that's nice Ma'am. I thought he would just be giving you a bible." Daisy smiled, and a sort of vacancy grew in her eyes. "Is there anything else you need from me Ma'am?"

"No thank you Daisy, just give Francis my thanks for the book. I mean Father Francis." Isabelle smiled

Daisy smiled at her and left, leaving Isabelle alone with her thoughts, and with her book. She sat at the edge of the bed; her hands

138

caressing the paper, each one in turn, as she carefully flipped the pages. Touching this book gave her the same chills that hearing Molly whisper to her in the night about her pretty mouth did. Isabelle closed her eyes and imagined Molly's lips, the way they felt like the underside of a rose petal, almost velvet. She remembers she pretended to be asleep when Molly kissed her, she was too afraid to move, to open her eyes, to ruin the only thing in her life that was beautiful. When she woke up the next morning Molly was gone, and she had never seen her again.

It was just a feeling of beautiful heartache, that day, and for the rest of her days, until now, until holding this book. She felt seen. She felt real. She held the book close to her as if it were a kitten, she looked down at it, and that was when she noticed a piece of paper, so much newer than the pages of the book. She opened the book carefully to the page. She removed the note that was there, and before reading it, she saw the underlined in faint pencil were the words *"He is more myself than I am. Whatever our souls are made of, his and mine are the same."*

Her hands shook as she read the note, just a few words scrawled on a torn sheet of paper, it read simply . . .

Isabelle ~ I've stolen the cinnamon buns, picnic in the morning. You can decide how many prayers I should say in penance for thievery. ~ Francis

Isabelle put the book down, and immediately got on her hands and knees and pulled the Hatbox out from under the bed. She lifted the hat gently as if it were a sleeping baby and placed the note underneath with the shell from yesterday. She put them all back where they belonged and slid the box back under the bed; directly under where she slept.

She took the teacup from her dining tray and walked to the window, opened it, let the bitter tinged liquid pour from her cup, when it touched the sea air, she could smell the sickness of it as it fell. It

139

smelled as if a mouse had died in an old pipe yet for some reason the water that ran from it was still consumed.

Chapter 20

Without help from various poisons, Isabelle's sleep was restless and fitful. The type of sleep you don't even realize is happening until you have woken, both startled and confused. Countless times throughout the night, she woke talking, seemingly startled out of what used to be everyday conversations. She would wake with the instant horror of Henry sleeping next to her, somehow covered in the stale blood from Oscar's birth, only to be overwhelmed with relief to find that she was alone.

The air seemed thick with an unnatural heat that radiated out from the deepest places inside of her, the place where her memories walked hand in hand with her nightmares. Her sweat smelled medicinal one moment, and like the musk of a fearful animal the next.

The one thing that remained constant through the night was the symphonic dialogue of relentless waves crashing onto the rocks, and what sounded like pacing and heavy stomping coming from what she could only assume was the attic above her. It sounded as if there was a shutter banging violently against the building, or perhaps a door slamming, or even the violent pounding of her own heart, as the beat is a disorienting rhythm inside her chest.

This went on for hours, as the night finally forgave itself and turned into day.

She arrived in the breakfast room rather late; she felt a surging of relief that she would not have to suffer through another ordeal with

Agnes and the piano. If anyone noticed her entrance or even her wild hair and pale skin, they did not make it obvious. It was as if the almost twenty-four hours since her "collapse" yesterday had never happened.

Patricia was staring delightedly at this morning's sticky pastry. She was counting each time she chewed, whispering her mantra into her teacup, letting it echo back to her like the phantom sounds of the ocean in a shell. Isabelle saw Francis sitting at a table in the middle of the room with several other men. He looked at her briefly, nodded once and went back to polite conversation. She was not sure, if he had seen her smile back, or if he had noticed the color coming back to her cheeks when she saw him.

She took a seat at the nearest empty table she could find. She heard a group of women as they filled with room with cackles like hyenas searching for prey. She heard Oscar crying somewhere just out of her reach. She heard young Molly whisper to her in the night, "You have the prettiest mouth I have ever seen." She opened her eyes in time to see Daisy place a breakfast tray in front of her. In the corner of the tray was a small folded piece of paper. She unfolded it and saw the words,

"Cathy~ Meet me at the gazebo, 10am. ~ Heathcliffe"

Isabelle smiled, less even at the invitation and more at the sense of being known. This simple understanding was the first thing in her life that was hers and hers alone. If she could somehow hold onto this feeling and turn it into something tangible, she knew she would hide it in the hatbox; she would want it protected.

Hidden.

She can't be certain what she ate that morning, but she washed it down with plain water that had had a dusty taste to it, as if it had been poured into glasses last night and left out to absorb the whispered sadness in the walls and the secrets of the night.

She looked outside; past the hunched over bodies who almost mindlessly put the food in their mouths, more out of habit than joy. She saw the sun breaking through the morning clouds and could see the robin's egg blue start to spread all the way to the Island and to her.

It would be the perfect day for a sun hat.

Isabelle could hardly wait to spring up from the table, feeling almost fully alive. The minutes passed slowly, as they did when she would be helping in the bakery and she would spend what now seems like years of her life wasting away in front of an oven. Whiling away hours just to have something be considered 'done'.

When breakfast was finished, Daisy rang a small brass bell, as if they were schoolchildren waiting for the end of day. Most got up in a slow lumbering fashion, but Isabelle, grabbed the folded note from her tray and exited with haste. She ran up the stairs holding her long heavy skirts in her hands. The weakness she felt earlier in her body was gone and replaced with the fluttering of baby birds showing their wings for the first time.

When she got to her room, she slammed her door not out of anger but out of unrequited excitement. She knelt on the floor with a heavy thud, landing on both her knees. She felt the tender skin of her pale legs, so rarely used; begin to split open a little as she knelt. She took her hatbox out from under the bed, tearing the lid off it and not with the tender care she showed before, as if she was afraid to wake the sleeping ghost, but instead as if she were ripping into a present that she had longed for. That beautiful bon voyage gift she had received before she was sent away. This was her crown; she was queen of this summer hotel.

She used her brush to try to tame her long near black mane of hair that had been growing wild in the damp air in the days she has been here. She could hear and feel the hairs ripping and breaking as she tried to find her way through the mass of storm waves and tangled seaweed that now lived on her head. Once she felt almost human again, she placed the beautiful straw hat on her head, the emerald green ribbon that adorned it wrapped around her face perfectly. The vibrant green against her dark hair was a startling contrast; it was almost inhuman. The dangling ends of the ribbon fell down her chest like tentacles. She could feel it, this hat on her head, calling to whatever it is that lives under the water, the thing that rears its head from the sea and cries out like a baby.

No.

No.

None of that is real. She tells herself. She reaches instinctively for a cup of tea to find nothing there to comfort her, there was only herself.

Isabelle went downstairs a little before ten and walked calmly through the foyer and out the front door. She tried her hardest to ignore the sleeping and cocooned women, waiting so patiently through their dreamless states finally to become butterflies.

Healthy and beautiful . . .

Yet now all they did was sleep and wait, for the chance to go home, perhaps. She did not know and if she were honest with herself as she would like to be, she would say that she didn't want to know.

As she approached the gazebo, she saw him before he saw her. He was sitting on a bench, head bent down. He sat with his shoulders rounded, and his posture seemed to be pushed down underneath an invisible but heavy weight. A burden. Isabelle could hear the way he said his "Ma," and she felt those words inside of her heart. She felt this for him, a heartache that felt like small stones being pushed inside you.

His coat was the normal black and though she could not see it, she knew the white collar would be there, screaming its lies at her as she tried with everything, she had to ignore it.

"You're early." She said with a brightness that though it seemed forced still rang like silver bells through the air.

"Oh, yeah it's a bad habit of mine. When you have nine sisters and brothers and you are smack dab in the middle of all of them, you learn if you want anything you need to get everywhere early." He said this and began to straighten his posture. She could see he did this with a bit of pain, as if realigning his bones to the proper order was a chore, a tortuous thing than most people take for granted. The way Francis moves it is as if each of his vertebrae were being stacked precariously on top of each other, a pile of stones that can easily topple despite its strength.

"Your hat is quite elaborate," Francis said with a teasing and easy good-naturedness underneath his words. Isabelle could tell he was a man who could put anyone at ease instantly, the sinners, the saints . . . and all the rest of them who did not know where they fit in with it all.

"Thank you, it was a gift." She said, almost as if she were apologizing for her feminine silliness of beauty seeking.

"It makes you look like a fancy sailing boat, or a tropical bird." He laughed as he said this, but it was not mean, in fact it had bordered on tender. She also realized as he said this that she had not seen him look directly at her.

"How dare you?" Isabelle laughed. "I rather like it, I feel fancy," she paused and then looked at him pointedly as she said, "almost like I'm going to church." She smiled. And as the breeze blew against her skin, she instinctively put her hand up to keep the hat on. It was still so new to her that she was not used to the wide satin ribbon holding it and framing it against her face, like the architecture of a church built on land often destroyed by war.

"I didn't say I didn't like it," he whispered. Again, it was almost as if he was on the opposite side of the confessional booth. "The green, it's beautiful against your skin. It's my favorite color actually." He looked down awkwardly and started to fidget and almost rewrap the food he had taken from the kitchen the night before, all of it sat wrapped in separate napkins in his lap. It was hammocked in with a

145

large piece of fabric, which appeared to be a woolen jacket that was going to be used as a picnic blanket.

Before she could ask what their plans were, he reached out and grabbed her near her wrist, and tugged her up from the bench, pulling her along with him. She let out a loud laugh, which was strikingly deep and boisterous. It erupted from her without any control, and though he made a shushing noise, she could see from the way the scar puckered above his lip that he was having fun.

He pulled her past the wooded trail she had taken the day before, and towards the back of the hotel and a road leading away and towards other houses and the water.

"I thought we weren't supposed to leave the property," Isabelle said, looking backwards towards the hotel as if they were being followed or chased.

"We're not, but you see I found these tide pools and they have the biggest snails I've ever seen; you need to see them in person, you'd never believe it." He was a little out of breath by this point, but before she could ask, he said, "Sorry, I can't go too fast. My lungs are shot, I had Tuberculosis when I was young, and that's when I was sent away the first time. Took years to get better, but I never got back to normal, not all the way." He slowed down a bit as they traveled further away from the hotel.

"Were you the only one to get sick, in your family?" She did not realize she had said it out a little loud until he looked at her.

His pace slowed a little more. "No, it killed two of my older brothers, and my baby, baby sister. No one recovered from that. Losing one that was so small," he paused, then whispered to whoever would hear him, "Sorry."

She could hear Oscar crying, as Francis said the words "baby, baby sister." As if his memory had called out to the ghost and everything that hurt inside of both of their souls woke up at once. She did not know why she said it, but she did. "His name was Oscar, my son. His name was Oscar. They did not want that to be on the grave or even on the birth certificate, so those things just said Baby Boy. But he had a name."

Francis turned to her, his cheeks flushed, and he struggled for breath, more than a man his age ever should have. "Well, I think that's a very fine name. You can tell just by having a name like that and a Ma like you, he would have turned into a good man. One you all could have been proud of."

Their walking slowed, and they strode next to each other. Isabelle could feel her skirt at times almost tangle between Francis' legs as they walked. Their hands never touched, yet the air beside them as they almost made contact sang with broken bits of hope, put together to form a song.

They continued walking onto a rocky path that began its strange and winding journey towards the rocky tide pools that lined the shore. He never reached for her hand to help her, even though the walk became slippery and precarious. He would however turn his head to check on her every few seconds, watching her as she placed her feet against the salted rocks. Making sure she was fine before he turned away again.

She thought at one point she saw his hand reach for her, but he pulled back at the last second. As if, he remembered their relationship should lack familiarity and the simple but beautiful intimacy of touching someone's hand when they need it is forbidden.

As they got closer to the shore, she could see the pools, their shallow waters shining in the late morning sun. She was careful where she stepped, not wanting to accidentally fall into one of the small underwater worlds. Surrounding her every step were these small sunken forests, little worlds she never imagined before today.

The tidal smell was strong, and she hoped that it would penetrate her skin and clothes; she wanted the magic of this moment.

147

She wanted it to become part of her; she wanted to smell like this day for as long as she could. Isabelle screamed out in laughter like a child thrown in the air to be caught at the very last second. She wanted this to be the memory of her life. To have this and not the rest of it be what she would remember when she finally closed her eyes for the last time.

She tried it now; she closed her eyes. She heard Oscar screaming, she heard, "you have the prettiest mouth I have ever seen," she felt Henry press himself into her that last time, when he told her not to fight, and in the end she thought she could feel the grundylow reach from these small beautiful ponds and wind its fingers around her ankles.

She opened her eyes and it all disappeared, all that was left was the sunlight, shattering the ponds into thousands of small paintings like the kaleidoscope Mother Minnie gave to Henry and Isabelle when they married. Henry found it pointless, but Isabelle fell in love with each imaginary world that was created with the mere winding of her hand.

"Isabelle you need to see this." She heard his voice calling her out of her reverent dreamlike state. She saw him then, as he tried to roll his pant legs up, his shoes already discarded on the driest rock he could find.

She realized then that she had walked out, almost precariously onto a rock almost surrounded by these small silent worlds at her feet.

Francis was unabashedly alive as he stepped his bare feet into these pools, unafraid that the small crabs would pinch at his skin. He seemed to have one goal in mind as he stepped with care, but no fear, into each of these pools. She heard his laughter as it traveled out of him, through the memories of her past and found her again, like a letter of love written in wartime and delivered many years too late.

"Isabelle . . .? Quick, I don't want to take him out of the water for too long." He shouted, not because the water was the same crashing loud cacophony that it usually was, but out of excitement.

The water here in this small enclave seemed far gentler, its low tide felt comforting, and almost invitational.

Isabelle traversed the rocks towards him, shoes still on, she lifted her skirts to protect them from the water, she did this out of a habit that had grown into her being like an invasive vine onto a house that is somewhere between rotting and collapse. She wished she could let the skirts fall off into the water; she wished her skin could feel the biting sting of the northern Atlantic.

She made her way to him; at this point he was almost knee deep in the second largest of the pools that she had seen. It was almost the size of a large man if he was laying down, arms and legs akimbo.

"Be careful!" Isabelle said, in between breathless laughter.

"Oh Jesus, this water, it's so cold it burns." Francis laughed and then coughed, as if both at the same time were nearly impossible for his lungs.

His back was to her, but as he was bending down into the pools, it began to soak his sleeves as his fished around in the water for something that seemed both elusive, and important. Isabelle felt a deep penetrating moment of fear that felt like the minutes before she went into labor for Oscar. She did not know what it was that Francis was looking for, but she knew it was for her.

He screamed out in delight, a sound of the earliest childhood joy as he pulled from the water something that looked at Isabelle's first glance, just like a tangle of urchins and moss.

"I tried to find a snail for you Isabelle, but this is even better." Francis turned to her with a smile so big that the scar that rode the trail from his lip to his nose was almost invisible. He held in his hand a strange colored orange fist, with its fingers wrapped around him, clinging for safety and comfort.

Isabelle's first instinct was to step back but seeing as she was precariously balanced on the wet rocks, she dared not move at all.

149

"What, what . . .?" She laughed, as if there was something in this moment that all of a sudden made her the person she could have been if her parents had not died, if she hadn't gone to almshouse. If there was no Henry, if there had been no Oscar. She in just mere minutes had started to become the person she could have been her entire life, someone who held onto happiness' hand, instead of scratching at it like an angry cat until it fled and hid under the bed.

"Put out your hands! Come on do it, make them nice and wide like a plate, I want him to stretch out." Francis was approaching her, and she had no escape. Her head was shaking back and forth, she was trying to say no, but her laughter took any ability to speak away from her.

She put her hands out in front of her with her palms up. She noticed for the first time in her life as her hands were pressed together, that the smallest finger on her left hand was so much larger than her other hand. She was lost in that realization when he placed the creature in her hands. Its five large legs seemed to stretch out onto her as if she was a chaise lounge. Now that it was not wrapped around Francis' hand so tightly, she could see its star like shape. The burnt orange color of it was the same color of the sky when day exhausts itself into sunset.

It writhed a bit, squeezing her hand and letting go, squeezing and letting go. She felt as if she was holding onto to something's heart. No, not a thing, a *who*, a someone. Someone's heart.

Her laughter stopped, and she looked at it. Francis' hand reached out, he let his fingers trace along the body of the starfish. Isabelle felt the creature grow slower; almost relax onto her. She got chills that raced up her back from the lowest part of her spine. These chills danced near the nape of her neck. She could hear Oscar finally stop crying, not because he died, but because he had exhausted himself to sleep. She heard Molly whisper next to her before she pressed her lips into her mouth.

Isabelle knew now that she should have not feigned sleep, that she should have opened her eyes to her friend when they were so young. Isabelle should have allowed herself to feel loved. Instead, she chose to feel alone. She did not know then, when she was still only a girl, that she would never have that sensation again, not until now.

Francis broke through her cloud of memories. "We need to put him back in the water Isabelle. He's fine for a few minutes, anything else is just cruel." He gently took the starfish from her; she did not look up, but could feel his eyes on her the entire time. The chills that danced at the nape of her neck began to fly like moths around the gaslight, so frantic in their exalted abandon that they never care when the tips of their wings singe under the heat of the flame.

Once the starfish was gone from her hand, and Francis gently placed him back in the same tide pool he came from, she could still feel the phantom of it in her hands. She thought that it would have been like that had she been able to hold Oscar. To feel his heartbeat, however, feint it might have been. She wished she could have felt it, his life. His three minutes of feeling loved.

They both had deserved that.

Chapter 21

She had been quiet after that. When he reached for her wrist, again, and not her hand, she let him guide her away from the slippery rocks onto a small of patch of grass closest to the jagged cliff of the shore. She heard him telling her that soon the tide would be coming in and all the pools would be under water. That they were the only ones today that saw into those little worlds and that by tomorrow they would all be different.

He untied the woolen jacket, it was a deep green color, and Isabelle was not sure if it was the unpleasant material or the color that made her think that it was a coat that had seen far worse things than a church confessional. This jacket had seen war; the fabric itself had absorbed the dying screams and cries of men, who in the end always ask for their mother. The coat cuffs were rough, frayed a little, and they still bore the dark maroon of old dirt.

Her hands touched the edges of it, almost as if she were picking it apart and trying to find out what was underneath it all. Francis reached out and moved the sleeves just out of her reach. "Oh, Isabelle, you don't want touch that and get your hands filthy, do you?"

Isabelle instinctively wiped her hands on her skirt, unsure if what she had been touching was dirt, or blood. She smiled politely and nodded her head. She was looking out at the water; she was already noticing the change in the current in just the ten minutes that it took to get where they were now. The water had grown so much more tempestuous. Its strengthening hands reaching onto the rocks and once again claiming what belonged to it.

The ocean was such an angry, selfish, and beautiful monster. It was as if it were a child that was once beloved and adored but as it grew up had become too strong, too beautiful, and too powerful to control. She loved it now, this untamed thing in front of her, almost as much as she feared it before she ever stepped foot on that boat.

"Why are we here?" she asked him. She was filled with yearning and dread for the answer.

"I'm not sure Isabelle, I thought you seemed like the type who would want to have some stale cinnamon rolls and watch the water with me." His smile was genuine, but his eyes whispered loneliness into the wind, until all it created were tears that he never let fall, not even as a child when the scar on his face was carved into him as if he was stone.

"You're awfully flirtatious for a priest." Isabelle joined Francis in his focus on the water instead of her.

"Oh, well, you know I'm not really a priest when I'm here. I'm just a man. Not even really a good one, I'm just a man." He paused while unwrapping the cloth napkins from the cinnamon rolls that were now two days past their prime. He handed one to her, without looking at her at all. She reached for it. There was a moment when their hands could have touched, but she instinctively drew back from that as if she were afraid of being burned. This small moment made her sink inside with the heavy stones of missed chances.

Isabelle blinked her eyes, the strong sea air making them tear up. She closed her eyes and felt comforted by the darkness in the strong almost summer light of mid-day.

"You have the prettiest mouth I have ever seen." It was Francis' voice and it was Molly's. They wound around each other until the fantasy and the memory were the same. Their voices whispered to her in between the ocean waves. If she could somehow dive between the thrashing water, she could find both of them. She could lean into that almost kiss, and let his fingers touch hers. Instead, she opened her eyes and once again chose the aching emptiness.

"So, you're not a good man, were you a good priest at least?" Her eyes crinkled a little when she smiled. She pretended that the water that edged out of her eyes were not tears, just a reaction to the salt on the wind.

"No, Jesus, I was a terrible priest. I don't believe in God, so that's a problem. I also don't know what happens to us when we die. I used to hope it was heaven, but now, now, I don't know what I hope. Sometimes I hope it's nothing; that we can just stop. That's why I'm here, I started saying this to people who wanted to hear a story about angels and I couldn't do it. So, they sent me here, to rest, to stare out day after day at God's fucking majesty." He gestured towards the water when he said the last part. He held the cinnamon roll in his hand, where a bible should have been.

"You could always leave, can't you? Your life doesn't need to be a lie." Isabelle said this, and the words danced between them. They played off the waves and she heard them again, but this time they were spoken for her.

"I can't do that," he said as he put a piece of the stale pastry in his mouth. His face took on a disgusted expression, and Isabelle was not sure if it was the food or the thought. "I made a promise to do this, and I can't break it. Besides, there are more lies than truths in here." Francis gestured towards his head. Isabelle wanted to ask him what he meant, but she knew she could not bear the answer, whatever it may be.

His expression went from turmoil to delight as he turned to look at her. His emotions seemed to shift so quickly without any warning like sunlight in a mirror blinding you one moment and sending you into shadow the next. He wiped the crumbs from his
155

fingers and reached out to her, and before she understood what was happening, he took the front of her hat and tugged it down over her eyes. She could hear his laughter, as she tried to get herself straightened out again.

"How dare you?" She smiled, again as they fell into a natural rhythm of just being together. She felt herself exhale and her shoulders drop.

"Let's play a game," she said to him.

"Alright, what's the game?" He seemed more relaxed now, but she thought he could teeter into darkness at any moment.

"Well, it's not really a game, but we ask each other questions, and the other person has to answer them, and it has to be truthful, no matter what. We have to swear to that." Her stomach fluttered in excitement and fear.

"That's not really a game Isabelle, that's just talking."

"No, when you're just taking you can always lie, but now we swear we won't." Her voice was more assertive now than she remembered it ever being during all her years as Henry's wife. Henry's forgotten object on a shelf.

"Alright, I'll start." Francis cleared his throat as if he were about to give a declaration or speech. "Where did you grow up?"

"I lived in Wells, Maine, near the water. A little place, not much bigger than the rooms we have at the hotel. After my parents died, I lived in an Alms House in Portland, Maine. It was close to a hospital, but we never went there, and there was an almost dried up creek close by. It smelled like rotting leaves, no matter what time of year it was . . . It's my turn now, so I'll ask the same thing."

"Well that's not fair," he said.

"No, you have to answer; it's what I want to know."

"I grew up for the first few years in Belfast; it's the northern part of Ireland. Not as pretty as people who have never been there might think, the streets smelled damp," he paused, trying to find the words, "and like metal that's rotted away. We came here, well to Boston, a neighborhood called Dorchester Neck, when I was about seven. Then after that, I ended up in Manchester, up in New Hampshire. I worked for Saint Anne's Church." Isabelle saw the small things in his face and voice that he probably did not realize screamed his truth. The fact that he said, "Saint Anne" with a sort of reverence, but then by the time he got to the word Church, the reverence turned to veiled sickness. "My turn . . . what is your favorite thing?"

"That's easy." Isabelle said, "It's this hat . . . and also today." She looked at him to gage his reaction. She studied him as if she were reading a foreign text that was somehow becoming clearer to her the longer, she stared at it. "What is your favorite smell?" She asked.

"Oh, that's easy, wet dirt." He laughed and then quickly asked his next question, trying not to diminish the energy between them, "What is your least favorite food?"

"Beef . . . I always thought it tasted like a cow crying." She expected him to look at her as if she was crazy, but he did not. He listened. "How did you know I would like the book you gave me? I never thanked you for that, I apologize."

He closed his eyes, as if he were trying to visualize or read the perfect response. *"I'm tired of being enclosed here. I'm wearying to escape into that glorious world, and to always be there: not seeing it dimly through tears, and yearning for it through the walls."* He stopped then, and looked at her. His eyes seemed to have a questioning look as if he could not remember the next line of the book. She knew though that of course he did, he knew them, and she began to feel that he knew her.

"Is that your answer, just quoting the book to me?" She asked, even though she knew that of course, that was his only answer.

157

"No . . . you can't ask two questions in a row. It's my turn. What is the worst thing you have ever done?" He looked at her, waiting to see the fight in her face. He looked expectantly at her as if he assumed, she would fight him, instead he saw her face relax and he just saw honesty.

"I didn't cry when my son died." She said it, in a matter of fact manner and quickly without letting the dust settle on her pain before she came back with her question. "How did you get the scar above your lip?"

"My father smashed his whiskey glass into my face when I had a nightmare. I think I was almost eleven." Francis looked at her with an expectation for her recoil, but instead he saw that she absorbed it fully even without a reaction. "Have you ever really loved someone Isabelle?"

It was the fact that he said her name that made her pause for a moment, almost unwilling to give this part of her to him, but she took a breath and said, "There was a girl, her name was Molly. I was young, and we were friends, but she was . . .," Isabelle didn't know how to put into words something that she only let linger on the edges of her very being. "She was what I thought happiness could have been. I haven't seen her since we were young, but there's not a day that goes by that I don't think of her, sometimes it's just a passing thought, and other times it takes the day away." Her words slowed at the end, as if this were the confessional and she finally whispered the secret that not even a priest understood how to pray it away. She let that linger there between them, before she asked, "How about you Francis, have you ever been in love?"

"I'm not sure. I think so, in my way. But you should ask me again when we are walking back to the hotel." She caught the corner of his mouth, turning upwards in an embarrassed grin as he looked away from her, and stared once again to the ocean. As they had been sitting there, the waves grew stronger and were swallowing the tide pools with their hungry power. It was as if those small under water worlds never existed at all.

"You don't know me Francis." She said the words even though her soul screamed that what she was saying to him was a lie. She knew in her heart that she should allow him to say the words out loud that everyone else around her had always been too scared to say or feel.

The truth was always a nightmare you woke from in the night. A thing that had terrified you but would still leave you with an ache somehow to get back to it.

"That's a fucking lie Isabelle and you know it. I know you. I've always known you. Way back when I was nothing more than these rocks and you were the water, coming close and then pulling away from me. It was out of both of our control . . . that's how long I've known you," he paused, looking at her briefly before turning back to the sea. "You're lying to both of us if you say anything different. You were meant to come here; we were meant to meet." His eyes glinted with a mania that only showed its bright shining form for a few moments at a time.

She wanted to fight it, this madness of his, but she could not. She knew it was true, and it scared her.

"For someone who told me you didn't have any faith, you sure so seem to have quite a bit of faith in this, don't you?" She said this and realized that her voice sounded almost sullen and angry.

"Yes, perhaps you're right. Maybe I haven't lost all my faith." He whispered it, loud enough for her to hear him, but she was not sure if that had been his intention. He grew quiet, as if the warm tender spell of the day had begun to frost over with the reality of it.

They sat there quietly for a while. Isabelle picked at the cinnamon roll that he had handed her earlier, but she found she did not have the stomach for it. She ended up breaking pieces off it and tossing them on the rocks below them. It was not long before there were close to a dozen sea birds fighting over the pieces of dried pastries as if they were the only thing between them and starvation. The caws grew louder until they seemed to be growing to a screeching cacophony. The sound made her back hurt, and her ears ring. She heard Oscar crying underneath them. She could almost imagine it was he being ripped apart below.

Isabelle let the rest of the food drop directly in front of her. She closed her eyes and clamped her hands over her ears. She felts the birds getting closer to her. Their wings beating against her skirts, they were like swimmers whose arms had grown tired and heavy after spending too long swimming against a current that would never falter in its strength. The strength of the bird's wings and the water would always keep her bobbing in and out. It would always keep her just on the verge of drowning.

She felt a sudden calmness wash over her; she no longer felt the birds as their wings beat ceaselessly against her legs. They had grown calm. She took her hands away from her ears, the only sounds she could hear were their beaks as they opened and closed making popping and clicking sounds. When she opened her eyes, she saw that Francis was feeding them, one at a time, and they patiently waited their turns. She heard his whispering in a chant, the words low and all seemed to blend in her ears at first.

It sounded holy, and private.

"I know you. I know you. I know you. I know you." He whispered these words, almost as if he was just exhaling, and truth, that nightmarish truth you long to succumb to, just happened to escape from inside of him.

Isabelle was not sure if the words were meant for the gulls, or for her. She reached her hands out and allowed her fingers to trace down a few of the bird's backs. They all seemed hypnotized, and hardly noticed her hands at all.

When Francis no longer had any food left, he opened his hands to the birds, showing them that they were empty and like a powerful unified force, one that reminded Isabelle of the soldiers when they marched through town headed south, the birds all flew at once back out over the water. The waves again drowned out their calls.

Francis brushed the crumbs from his lap as he stood up, this time he reached for her hand without saying a word. She realized his skin was rough, as if he were in fact still made of those same stones they were sitting on. They walked silently back towards the hotel, hugging the shadows of the mammoth building the entire time. They were children hiding during a game that their parents never fully realized they were playing, and they were soldiers hiding from an enemy who seemed to know them better than they knew themselves.

He only let go of her hand as they rounded to the front of the veranda. The women were lined up and still sleeping on their chairs, like stone statues on an old castle. Behind their sleeping eyes, there could always be spies. Isabelle saw one of them, seeming to shift self-consciously as she heard footsteps approaching on the gravel path, her eyes opened briefly and then closed again. It was young Agnes, the pianist, and though Francis walked ahead of her by many feet, there was no disguising that they had been retuning from someplace together.

Isabelle walked with tenderness up the large wooden steps towards the front door, the same way she would sneak through her house under a cloud of laudanum, grief, and fear. She was two steps from the top when she heard the wooden step let out a moan. The wood itself warped like all of them under the weight of time and salted air.

Agnes' eyes popped open immediately and fixated on Isabelle who was now the only one on the veranda. The look on the young girl's face was a combination of jealousy, and a deep seeded bloom of mockery that grew over her face like vines. Agnes let that look grow between them until it almost bloomed. She then leaned back on her

161

chair and closed her eyes as if whatever it was that made her alive inside had been turned off. She was once again a sleeping doll with a decaying rose petal for a mouth.

Isabelle walked into the lobby to find Francis there, waiting for her. He had not said a word to her since they were sitting on the rocks, which was already beginning to feel like a memory, or a wish.

He looked around the room quickly to make sure they were alone before he took her hand again. This time it was just the tips of her fingers. He held her delicately, as if she were glass very recently glued back together. All her seams were still wet and could come apart with the slightest of unwanted pressure.

"Be careful of her Isabelle," he said, again his eyes darting. She was not sure if it was out of protection for her or paranoia. "There is something not right about her."

"There's something not right about all of us here," Isabelle said, with a strange solidarity towards all the women here, she felt in defending their honor and sanity she was defending her own.

"Not her, she doesn't belong here, she belongs someplace else. Her family, they . . . He stopped, and looked at her; he tried to communicate something but could not. "She belongs in a hospital, a real one." Again, his eyes darted around the room. Isabelle's fingers that at first, so delicately resting in his hand was now being gripped. His overall demeanor made him look like a cat that young boys on the street would corner in an alley and throw rocks at.

"It can't be that bad Francis; they wouldn't let her be here if she was dangerous." Isabelle said this, and she could hear the naivety in her voice, her misbegotten innocence tasted the way lilacs smelled when they had been left too long in the same jar. Her words and thoughts, like the flower, began to go bad from the inside out. The flowers were still beautiful, and seemingly healthy, but the water and green leaves that were their very essence, began to smell of the deep rot of a phantom swamp.

162

"She shot her father, actually, and not for any reason, she just wanted to. She's proud of it. She's lucky she didn't kill him." He said with the anger of men. It was in his very core the way it was in all of them, even the very best of men.

"I don't think she would have shot him for no reason," Isabelle said, again defending not just Agnes, but all of them. When she said this, she could feel the weight of Henry on top of her, when it would have been better if she *didn't fight it*. She felt the fingers of a different priest so long ago when she was just a child at the Almshouse. She looked him in the eyes as she said, "We always have a reason for what we do."

"Just be careful," he said, his back already turned to her, as he walked towards the locked liquor cabinet that sat like a stoic soldier near the piano. Isabelle felt that his quest would be fruitless, until she saw him pull a key out of his pocket and open it with authority. It was as if he was not a guest there at all, it was as if he was part of this place.

In this whisper of a moment, he seemed like her enemy *and* the only person she could trust.

Chapter 22

In the dining room, on the night of their picnic, Francis and Isabelle treated each other as if they were intimate strangers. The only time they looked at each other was when the other one had already turned their head. They filled the hour by staring out the large glass windows into the endless alone of the ocean. Isabelle moved the food around her plate with sense of making it look as though she were believably eating.

The only difference between this night, and the ones that had preceded it, was that they could feel each other. There were unspoken scars on their insides that were being cut open, stitch-by-stitch with each unanswered look. Isabelle felt like a fancy dress that was poorly made. The different parts of her were separating and being held together by straight pins. If she moved the wrong way in her mind, she would feel them stick into her pale skin. She would bleed. She would lean into the sound of his voice as it traveled across the room. She could swear that if she concentrated that she could feel his shadow against hers. Pushing and pulling at her like the tides.

They had an invisible world that lasted one day. It was a tidal pool that would never exist again. Any living thing scuttling along the bottom of its shallowness had been swept out to sea. The living things that came together for one brief afternoon no longer existed now in the world they had to share with the others.

The endless dinner party of the absurd.

As Isabelle went to her room that night, she found herself remembering the gull's wings as they beat against her skirt. She could feel Francis' hand as it held her fingers gently and grew stronger with fear. Isabelle, alone now, moved her fingers to her lips and she traced the curves of her mouth and remembered Molly's words. She would remember Molly's kiss, but soon that memory of Molly faded, and it was Francis. Isabelle licked her lips and savored the salty taste that seemed to increase when her lips cracked. They had grown dry and raw from the air and the sun.

Her sleep that night was fitful and restless, if there was any sleep at all to be had. She tossed restlessly and tore at her sweat soaked sheets in an almost feverish delirium. She could feel herself fade into this wasteland between sleeping and awake. She could feel her body become heavy and she was unable to move. That was when she would hear it the loudest.

The cries. They became a wall of sound; surely, this was more than just Oscar's ghostly wails. She could hear the stomping of footsteps overheard, and on stairs going up and going down.

Pacing.

Stomping.

Creak.

Thud.

Creak.

Then as soon as she thought she would not be able to take it any longer, there was only silence, there was just her heartbeat as it began to slow. Not even her breath made any sounds.

Still, she was unable to move. In fact, there were times that she felt the air had almost been pushed out of her. She would come to, gasping for breath, and first only able to move her fingers. She was not awake, or asleep.

She was not alive, and she was not dead. She thought she could hear a whisper from the darkest parts of the corners of her room saying, "look at me . . . look at me . . ."

She finally gasped for air as if she had been half drowned, and she sat up in bed, released from the paralysis that she had been stricken with for minutes.

Maybe longer.

She looked at the small clock by the bed, and saw that it was coming up on three am, and though she knew the sun rose early over the water that it would still be hours before the comfort of daylight could assuage these feelings of unrest.

She was tired.

She was more tired than she thought she was; Henry was right. Mother Minnie was right.

She got up and paced through her room, when her feet hit the cool wooden floor, they felt almost wet, as if she was standing in the tidal pool from earlier. If she stopped pacing for a moment, she could feel her feet grow warm against the wood. She could imagine the water warming around her in the sunlight. The air around her cloyed with heavy salt air. If she moved her feet, she was sure she would see puddles underneath her.

She was startled to hear what she at first thought was her door opening and slamming shut. She turned to face her door, assuming that she would see someone else in her room with her, but there was nothing, she was alone, except for the Oscar, he had to be close, his cries grew louder.

She walked to her door, in a quiet and creeping manner, as if she were the one trying to sneak up on someone unannounced. She opened her door; it made a sound like an exhale. She was taken a back at how disarming the long hallway looked at night. The rows of closed doors on either side of the long stretch of this east wing led itself almost seamlessly all the way to the other side of the hotel. The only thing that was there to greet her was the large window at the far end of the hall. It stared out across the part of the Island she had never seen. Of course, at this hour she could only see darkness, a black gaping maw. It seemed to her that the window was the mouth of a monster, and inside of that monster was the island. It was a landscape that she never had seen, even though it was so close, it was to her, a terrifying stranger.

The symmetry of the hallway, the closed doors and the dim greenish lights of the oil lamps that still burned through the night but were turned down almost to nothing, made her feel dizzy, and unsure. She closed the door of her room behind her. It made a small sound like a velvet box being closed with precision and care. She was not sure if there were rules about walking through the hotel at night when everyone should have been sleeping.

She walked down the hallway, letting her hand trace against the wall and all the closed doors that she passed. She felt like a child who was afraid to be lost in the woods, even though the hallway was a straight line, that she would somehow never find her way back to where she belonged.

She made it to the center staircase in silence. It was then that she heard what sounded like footsteps above her, running the length of the hotel in a haphazard and panicked pattern. The noise had to be coming from the attic, or the servant's quarters. It had to be. She heard the running again, the stomping. It made Oscar's ghostly cries ring out even louder. It was joined in tandem with others, as if all the children in the house were woken at the same time.

No, there are no children here.

She was told that the first day she was here.

The second day she was here, she found the graves.

No, there are no children here.

Yet still, she did hear the crying.

She turned deliberately back towards her room. Taking stock of the doors she passed, her hand feeling the same wooden inlay on each of them. Isabelle took comfort in the sameness of it all. They were sleeping soldiers. Sleeping broken dolls . . . that is, until her hand traced against a door and there was no inlay, at least not where it was supposed to be. She took her hand away quickly as if it had leaned against the oven door for a moment too long. She took a step back and looked at it.

It was subtle, the difference in this door from the others. It had the same decorations, the same inlay. It was just about six inches lower than the rest. The height and width of this door was just that much smaller all around. She looked at the doorknob and noticed that the wood was unpolished, unlike the rest of the doors.

This door seemed to be screaming into the ocean air that it should not be looked at, not be noticed. No, this door was unimportant.

She told herself it was the servants' quarters. That if she opened the door, she would find Daisy, and Nora and the two young men that carried the bags. The running was surely them, having a game, after all the guests were asleep. After all, they really were only children themselves. They deserved it. The running and stomping did not seem to be a bother to any of the other guests.

She started to walk away, but then at the last moment decided to reach out, she wanted to touch the doorknob. Feel the unpolished wood. She thought that perhaps it would remind her of the almshouse. She hoped when her fingers touched the wood, she would hear Molly's voice, and feel her lips against hers. Yet when her hand connected with the knob, she could hear only Oscar; his screams were that of a terrified baby. Though she had never been allowed to see him, she could almost imagine his small face, turned red, his little hands, reaching out to her.

Without thinking, she opened the door to find only a steep stairwell that went almost straight up, more like a ladder than stairs at all. They curved towards the left after about ten feet, and what came after that, Isabelle didn't know. She climbed the stairs, placing her hands on each of the risers above her head and almost pulling herself up. The light from the hallway began to fade, but not before she noticed that, the stairs were caked with a thick layer of dust and old hair clinging to the corners. As she rounded the curve of the stairwell, her eyes began to adjust to the darkness. The only light seemed to come from the moon as it reflected off the water and made itself up here, penetrating the windows that seemed at first glance to be opaque with the filth of many years of neglect.

It appeared that she was wrong; this was not the servant's quarters at all. At the top of the stairs she found herself in another hallway, this one seemed to be much smaller than the long corridors of the main hotel. This one running perpendicular to what was downstairs. This hallway ran the width of the hotel and not the length. She could barely make out the end of the hallway and saw that it curved to the left at the end.

In front of her, she saw three doorways, of what must be small cramped rooms. The doors were all open and the hallway was filled with boxes and debris. Years of the hotel's past were locked away in old cardboard boxes that seemed to be water stained, and smelled not like the sea, but instead like a stagnant swamp and the urine of rodents.

She stepped over the boxes carefully trying not to touch anything. She could feel the bottoms of her feet that only a short while ago felt cool and wet, now felt thick with the dust of forgotten memories.

She was able to make her way to the first small room, barely more than a closet. It was filled with bassinets, and cradles. Every

170

surface of the floor was covered with them, as if they were placed together in an intricate puzzle, the kind that she was always so terrible at when she was young.

Her breath seemed to catch in her throat, her hands started to shake. She stood in the doorway, frozen in time like an effigy of a long-forgotten saint. She took a step backwards before remembering how close she still was to the steep ravine of the stairs. She heard nothing. Even Oscar ceased his plaintive cries. She pressed on towards the second doorway, stepping over the boards that felt rotted and soft under her feet.

She could see inside this one before she got to the doorway. The cradles, bassinets, and cribs were all stacked on top of each other, at least three high. They seemed to be on a base of small child sized beds, which were made of cast iron. When she was young, she and the other children at the almshouse would call them orphanage beds. She reached her hand to touch one of the cribs that was precariously balanced towards the top but just before she was able to touch it, she heard a creak from the room next door. She put her hand down immediately as if her movement was forcing an alarm to go off. She held her breath.

She thought she could hear the faint almost indecipherable hum of a lullaby. Then, there was another creak, and then another.

It was not creaking so much, as it was a rocking. It sounded like a chair, a rocking chair. Similar to the one that Henry had bought for Isabelle before Oscar was born. She of course, never sat in that chair with him, but during her long laudanum filled days, would often find herself standing over that chair rocking subtly and then having it grow in ferocity like a tempest. She remembered the way the chair would sound, as it would bang into the wall of her bedroom.

That was it of course, the same sound she heard over her head at night. The slamming, it was not a door slamming; it was a rocking chair hitting the wall in repetition.

Oscar began to shriek inside her head, inside the very walls of this hotel, he was determined, this boy of hers. His sounds were guttural, the types of noises you make you make when you think there is nothing left for you. She has made those noises herself; she recognized her voice in his. His screams sounded like he was calling out for her. She had to go to him.

She walked the rest of the way down the small and cluttered hallway. Though the floor was littered along the way, she noticed a labyrinthine path through the chaos that leads her here. The first few steps she took she could hear the humming and the rocking. As she grew closer, it stopped.

Isabelle stood a few feet away from the door when she heard someone stand up, and the weight of the chair slam into the wall behind it. She took a few more steps, she half expected to turn the corner and see herself standing there, holding baby Oscar as he squirmed in her arms.

However, it was not her.

She knew her right away, though her face was turned away from the door towards the window. The moonlight shone on her face in just the right way, cutting Agnes' features into two, a light and a dark. As she turned her face towards Isabelle, she fell completely into shadow. The thing in her arms, wrapped so tightly in a blanket seemed to squirm for freedom. Whatever it was, it made a sound like a cat that was being squeezed too tightly around its throat. Agnes squeezed the writhing blanket until there was one small guttural sound and then silence.

It was then that Oscar finally stopped screaming.

Isabelle let her breath out in a strangled gasp. Agnes brought her hand to her mouth and with her index finger let out a, "Ssshhhh."

Agnes smiled then, for the briefest of moments before she dropped the now dead cat to the floor of the room.

Isabelle did not know if Agnes was following her, but she tore down the hallway through the newly defined path through the debris of memories. When she got to the stairs, she backed down them as if she was going down a ladder. Her bare feet barely seemed to touch the stairs on her way down. Her toes seemed to slide down, connecting with the air more than any of the landings.

By the time she backed into the hallway of the hotel, she felt as if she were thrown into a different world. She rushed to the closed door of her room, her hand twisting at the polished doorknob to find that it was locked . . .

She remembered her first day there, being told that none of the doors locked, for the guest's protection. It did not make sense; the hotel itself was lying to her. She backed away from the door, running down the hall towards the main staircase. She kept turning her head staring at not only her locked door, but also the open door of the attic. If Agnes were following her down the stairs, she could not hear it over the thunderous sound of her own heartbeats and her near hysterical gasps for air to fill her lungs.

She did not see him, before her body ran directly into his. Unlike herself and even Agnes, Francis was not in nightclothes. Instead, he was dressed as he always was, the dark pants, dark shirt and jacket, and the white collar. The starkness of it almost hurt Isabelle's eyes when she would look at it.

The sound that escaped from Isabelle's mouth was a frantic, gasping bellow. It was cut short by Francis' hand as it clasped just slightly too hard over her mouth to stop her scream. His left arm had curled around her waist, as if they were sweethearts who would dance too close to each other whenever their chaperone would look away. His right hand was the one clasped over her mouth. While having his hand there certainly muffled her cries, it did not stop them. He repeatedly made quiet shushing noises, which unbeknownst to him, only served to antagonize Isabelle more, as she remembered Agnes making the same sound minutes before.

173

She was able to look directly into his eyes, and saw they were the same as they were earlier, while they were sitting on the rocks by the water. Though she had no idea if she could trust him, she knew that what he was doing right now was for her protection.

His head turned slowly towards that open attic door, and she saw fear wash over him. He held her just a little tighter around her waist and the pressure of his hand against her mouth began to become lighter. She could feel her initial panic begin to fade, as her breath began to escape from between his fingers. Her lips trembled against his calloused hands. Inexplicably she began to shiver, not from the cold, but from adrenaline.

Isabelle's head turned as well and she followed his gaze to that open attic door, they stared at it in anticipation. There was a calmness to him, as if he were reading a story that he has always known the ending to. They stood there in silence, as a slender white arm reached out from the hidden stairwell. It grabbed the unpolished doorknob and closed the small door.

He took his hand away from her face and took her by the arm back towards her room.

"It's locked; I tried to get in before," she said, her voice barely above a whisper. She was still out of breath, panting as if she had run a great distance, or felt the crushing cold of a Northern Atlantic wave crash into her chest.

"The doors don't lock Isabelle, you know that." Francis reached for the doorknob and opened the door with ease. He walked into her room, still holding her by the arm. He reached for her gas lamp and turned the light up. It cast unnaturally long shadows of each of them. These shadows stretched across the room towards each other and seemed to almost quiver and move before Francis and Isabelle did.

Francis let go of her arm, reached for the pitcher of water, poured her a glass, and handed it to her. He in turn reached for the flask in his pocket.

"I think I would rather have that," Isabelle said, as she gestured towards his whiskey. He handed it to her and let her take a sip. His eyes were locked on her the entire time. She began to feel self-conscious and thought at first of taking a small 'delicate sized ladies sip'. Though when she felt the warmth of the alcohol in her mouth, she realized she was no longer shivering, and took another longer pull.

"I told you to stay away from her," Francis said, his voiced was filled not with anger but with an overly exhausted amount of concern.

"I didn't know she was up there," Isabelle said.

"But why were you up there Isabelle? Why?" He reached for the flask again and took it from her in a way that was rough with anger that masks fear. His hands were noticeably shaking more now than they were a few minutes ago.

"I heard something, I don't know why I went up there, I just did. Why was she up there? She had a cat . . ." Isabelle's voice trailed off a bit at the end, as if she thought that her words made even less sense than her memories.

"She takes care of it; she thinks it's her daughter . . . Wait did you say had?" Francis looked at Isabelle and then suddenly looked towards her door. She could almost read his mind; he was worried. He looked like an animal in the hour before a thunderstorm. He was anxious and unsettled.

"She killed it when she saw me. Maybe she did not mean to. It was moving, making sounds. She grabbed it so tight, squeezing, and twisting its neck." Isabelle reached again for the flask, which he handed her as if they were sharing secrets back and forth.

"Jesus," he said, as he hung his head. He sat down on the edge of Isabelle's bed, looking defeated. She remained standing, backing herself almost against the glass of her window. The coolness of which made her heart begin to slow to a near normal rhythm.

"You said she had a daughter? Where is she?" Isabelle asked, but she already knew in her heart that the answer lay in the piles of fresh dirt in the hidden away graveyard.

"Oh Isabelle, she died. The baby died." He sighed and lifted his head, checking on Isabelle to make sure she would be fine hearing those words.

"How did the baby die? And when?" Isabelle's voice was beginning to raise, not only in volume but also in octave.

Francis sighed, not wanting to look at her, his head faced up towards the ceiling, or towards his long-abandoned God.

"She was born wrong, she died." He said this with a determination in his voice; as if he were stopping a conversation that he knew in his heart could not be stopped.

"How do you know all of this?" Isabelle asked and inside she braced herself for an answer she knew she did not want to hear but knew she needed to. Isabelle did not want to admit to herself that she feared that he would tell her he was the father of this young girl's, young girl.

"Oh, fuck . . . Isabelle." He sighed once and his shoulders dropped. "Agnes and I, we're lifers here. I've been here three summers; she has been here for all of those, maybe more. She comes early, before most of the guests, before the season starts. Twice she was pregnant when I got here." He stopped. He shook the near empty flask and could hear a small amount of liquid still swimming at the bottom. He drank the rest of it, tilting his head all the way back and pouring the last drops into his mouth. "The babies always die. They're born wrong, and even if they weren't, they shouldn't live. Not for their own sake or even for hers . . . They're an abomination."

"Her father, he rapes her?" Isabelle asked, understanding what she thought was the puzzle pieces she was meant to put together.

"You see, that's the problem, she doesn't see it that way. Her mom died when she was a young."

"She's still young," Isabelle interrupted. "It's why she shot him . . . you wouldn't tell me before," She said.

"Oh yeah, she shot him because love is a funny thing." He said this with a sneer.

"No, that's not love."

"Oh, and you know everything about love don't you Isabelle. Sometimes love is ugly, and sick." This time it was Francis' turn to interrupt her.

"How do you know all of this? I know you're close to Mister Hughes, did he tell you this?" She wondered, understanding now that she still did not know all the parts of the story.

"Do you really need me to say it Isabelle?" He stopped and waited for Isabelle to respond, but she did not. She just pressed herself closer into the cool glass of her room; it looked as though she could just lean back and be gone for good. "I know because Hawthorne wanted someone for the funerals." He said this and his voice rattled with thick shame.

A coldness crept over Isabelle, a sort of disconnection of herself and her feelings. She did this a lot when she was younger and found that it was her most useful talent that she had ever cultivated.

"I thought you were here because you were like the rest of us. I thought you were *tired*," she said, her voice lower again, in her normal husky range, the ice in her words made them come out less like a whisper and more like a hiss.

"I am tired Isabelle," he said, as if he had been defeated.

"I thought you said you were here because you stopped believing in God." She did not know why she was so angry about the thought of Francis being at the funeral for these countless unnamed children. She thought of Oscar, how he had no funeral, no name. None of it seemed fair. She knew she should be angry, so she was.

"I don't believe in God," he said. The defeat in his voice became colored on the edges with pride.

Isabelle closed her eyes; she thought of Oscar, his small body buried somewhere that she would probably never know about. There was no place to visit, no headstone with his name, and no small pile of dirt to hold in her hands; to fill her pockets with, to take home with and place it somewhere special. She realized now that Oscar had stopped crying. He was angry too, with her, for her, maybe even at her.

She took a deep breath and looked at him with little emotion on her face or in her voice. "I want you to get out of my room."

"I didn't have any other choice Isabelle; I had nowhere else I could go."

"I don't care. I want you to leave. I'm tired. Agnes will probably be playing the piano soon."

"Isabelle . . ."

"Look, we had a perfect day together. I was happy. The happiest I might ever have been. But that is done now, and I want you to go." It was with those words that the tears started in her eyes, and rather than let him see her, she turned her head and faced out the window. The horizon was just beginning to glow out over the water. The yellow haze would weigh heavy over the island until late morning. As if this night would refuse to release its hold on all of them. She didn't know how she knew it, but she could feel it like a dull ache in her bones.

She could just make out the reflection of her door opening and closing as Francis left. She was finally alone, without even Oscar's continuous howl for company.

Chapter 23

The days flowed in and out of each other as water poured from pitcher to glass and back again. If Agnes remembered anything about being discovered in the attic, she never let on. She played the piano twice daily. She smiled and charmed her way through all the guests, weaving in and out of them like fine fibers being woven into something sacred.

Isabelle could hear her in the attic at night, but she never went back to check on her. She thought she could detect on one of the hotter and more humid days, a faint aroma of animal decay as she walked down the hallway towards dinner one evening. She chose to ignore it. She wondered if there was a new cat in the attic with Agnes, to take the place of her ghost children.

Isabelle was kept awake for nights on end, with the footsteps that seem to run and pound over her head, and the creaking of the rocking chair as it moved back and forth in an almost hypnotic rhythm. The sounds that made the hotel seem haunted, she knew now were from the ignored and imaginary world that Agnes inhabited existing above her.

Oscar's cries became all but relentless and seemed to come from the walls that surrounded her, no matter in what room she was. The consistency of his phantom wails began to soothe her, much like she supposed Agnes' rocking chair did for her. It was the way the ocean waves and the ever-present tea, did to the others. His wails would grow powerful throughout the night, screaming a cacophony of loneliness and hunger.

She loved that these cries of his no longer stopped after three minutes that they went on and on as if he were a child that never ran out of breath. These sounds held and rocked her through the night until she almost grew sick with the constant motion of it. He was a threatening sky hanging low and heavy over the water. His cries would make the ocean swell and become violent, yet it would never give itself over and become a storm.

This lasted the entire summer, through all the endless days and the nameless hours.

Isabelle began to realize that her time here in this hotel existed only because the rest of her reality had burned away with morning fog.

The few times during the night that she allowed herself to let Oscar fade into a subtle hum, she was able to sleep. His cries became summer memories that sounded like cicadas in the tall grass. She could exist there, in this . . . in between, a place of memory, half hallucination and loneliness. She would find herself missing Francis. She could feel the memory of his hand, and it was almost real. She would remember it this way . . . pretending that her fingers were his, or they were Molly's. She would wile away the hours in between both of their memories. She would fall into a pantomimed happiness until she would sit up in bed startled as their hands turned cold, twisted, and gnarled. Her heart would beat heavy and uneven in her chest as she realized that their fingers had turned into the gnarled driftwood of the grundylow's fingers. Her fear could not stop the creature from reaching into her bed and creeping its way under her sheets and inside of her.

She would lay back down, her head hitting against the pillow as if she had fallen on ice. She would be almost relieved . . . at least then she was not alone.

At times, she was comforted by the presence of this unreal thing that was with her in that dark room. Its demonic fingers would soil the all too crisp white sheets. The sheets that were so stiff and pure that they seemed to cut at her skin like nettles on sun bleached and dried grass. The moisture of these imaginary fingers would make the bed begin to seem soft, and wet. Those phantom fingers began to be a comfort in the night.

She would allow this imaginary phantom to touch her. It would start out as Francis before turning to Molly, and then back to Francis again . . . if she allowed herself to hope and to dream it would only last so long before it would always eventually decay and rot until all she could hear was the memory of Henry's whispers that, "it would be better not to fight it." In her nightmares, Henry and the grundylow feel the same when they enter her.

This is when Oscar's crying would ramp back up; held away by nightmares for only so long.

Sometimes in the darkest and most labyrinthine moments of the night, she could see the corners of her room begin to peel away. She imagined that someday she would live behind the walls, and there would be someone else in this bed, feeling her fingers in the night.

Isabelle started to drink the tea again. She was sure it was not helping, but it couldn't be making things worse. The world around her started to shred, like the edges of a handkerchief worn thin from too many years of hidden grief. It began to come apart at the seams.

She was tired. She would whisper towards her ceiling in between muffled giggles and tears, "I'm more tired than I think I am Molly." Isabelle would close her eyes and wait for Molly's kiss.

It never came.

She would show up to breakfast, beaten and broken from a night of torment. The sleeplessness becoming the very thing with what she shared her meals. When she would dare to look at Francis, she had seen that he too, had grown gaunt. The fire that had lived in his eyes was no longer there, it had been snuffed out. All along, Francis had just been fire that was trying to be started with moldering wood. He was a flicker of something, and then he was not. The thing that had been special inside him had grown heavy and made him seem as if he was being bent from the inside. He was a crooked man. She thought she could remember a rhyme about that . . .

Isabelle began to spend her afternoons, not dozing in a medicated slumber on the chairs with the rest of the pale and broken dolls, but instead sitting on the front steps to the hotel. She would spend her time leaning against the pillar that held the potted flowers, different ones arriving fresh every few days with the newest guests.

The flowers that had grown wilted and rotted around the edges would be taken away. No one wanted this place to seem unseemly. No one wanted the decay to be seen from the dock as the guests made their way to the hotel for the first time.

So many seemed to arrive, but none of them ever seemed to leave. The bags of mail also grew smaller by the day. As if families back home had grown tired of writing words on pieces of dead trees, just to be responded to with handwritten scrawls of riddles and rants.

Henry never wrote, not once. Mother Minnie sent a letter sometime at the beginning of July. It was a short note, telling her she hoped she was healing. HEALING was written in all capital and printed letters. The rest of the envelope was filled with cut out recipes and a pattern for a new skirt that seemed to be ripped, not even cut, but ripped out of Frank Leslie's Ladies' Magazine.

Isabelle wanted immediately to take these things and throw them into the ocean, but then, thinking better of it, she stuffed them into one of the pots of flowers, before it was taken away and replaced with something new.

Something fresh.

Something healthy.

She was too afraid to stay inside all day, but she feared she would flutter out like a flame if she stepped more than a few feet away from the building. She grew suspicious of the sunlight touching her skin. It scared her, but not as much as the long shadows of the hotel, and the even stranger ones from the guests.

She told herself she was not sitting there waiting for Francis. She also told herself that she was not there to bear witness to the comings and goings of that little path past the gazebo. The one that led to the freshly dug little graves she had found that first day.

She thought about those miniature graves, those small piles of dirt, the markers carelessly placed there with no names. Were they all children? Were some of them pets? Was Agnes' strangled cat now sleeping there with her daughter? She would lose herself in the confusion between the two. The only thing that would shake her out of it would be the memory of when she heard Francis' voice say that his favorite smell was wet dirt, and she wondered at how many of these small ceremonies he had taken part. How much of that wet dirt was from this place?

After weeks of sitting there on the step, sipping her tea when it was given to her, staring into the day with seemingly blank eyes, she grew bored.

Restless.

Her hands wanted to do something more, they wanted to reach for a hand that was not there. They wanted to turn the pages of that book that was hidden away in her room. She wanted to hold her son. A memory she was never allowed to have. If she thought about it enough, she could feel a book page under her fingers. She could feel Francis' hand as it held hers. She could feel Molly's mouth, like a moth about to turn to dust against her lips. She had felt those things; they had been experienced in her life.

When she thought of holding Oscar, there was nothing.

Her hands could reach for him through all her memories and still they would come back wanting. She waited for a small hand to reach out to her, grasp around her finger. She could almost imagine the slightest bit of pressure that an infant's love could express on her hand.

She could imagine it, but she could not feel it. She could not remember it. It never happened and it never will.

When her imagined memories could no longer satiate her, she spent her days peeling away at the chipped dirty white paint of the wood that she leaned against for comfort and stability. She would peel the sharp edges of the roughest part of the stairs until underneath all her fingernails were filled with splinters that began to swell as they became infected over these hot mid-July days. She wanted to scream out with the pain of it, but she held it in, and continued to pass her time with this incessant peeling.

Her fingers would throb with each of her heartbeats. The skin under her nails would pulse as if it were alive. To keep from screaming she would put her fingers in her mouth. They tasted like old paint covered in salt and pollen. They also tasted like copper. That was the blood. She thought the more she peeled away at the wood the easier it would be to eventually be able to tell what kind of tree it was, that made the stairs, this railing. Was it Oak, Maple?

Isabelle always hated the outdoors, but suddenly she was convinced that she would be able to taste the history of the trees in the blood as it collected under her fingernails.

It took almost a week before anyone noticed what she had done to herself. The only person who took notice of her hands was Daisy. Once she saw them, the maid put away the rag she was polishing the banister with, took Isabelle by the arm, and promptly brought her into the kitchen. She let her sit on a high stool near the stove. Daisy poured nearly boiling water in a small bowl before she added salt and a few drops of an oil that smelled faintly exotic and pungent; the way a lagoon must have smelled when it all but runs dry in the longest parts of a summer.

Isabelle was able to soak her fingers in that scalding water and watch Daisy and Nora prepare food for people who never bothered to thank them. For people who barely bothered to know where they were. Isabelle would spend time in the kitchen, soaking her wounded hands every afternoon before teatime.

Her days became ritualistic in their monotony.

Breakfast

Tea.

Stairs.

Hands.

Tea.

Dinner.

Tea.

Bed.

All the while the crying never stopped, no matter how much she wanted to rest. Oscar cried. She thanked him for that, every day, her constant companion.

The hotel seemed almost filled by the end of July, and Isabelle began to feel as if she was fading out of this world a little more every day. At this rate, she would be invisible by the end of summer. Perhaps that was what Henry had wanted all this time.

It was as if she had never come back from the picnic that day. When she looked back on it all, her memories bore a haze of nostalgia and a bittersweet ache. That day seemed so long ago. She remembered clinging to the shadows of the hotel with Francis, as if they were children playing a game. She wondered if she had come back more shadow than woman.

Even now when she looked at Francis it seemed like he too was fading away, growing blurry, as if her eyes were tired, and he was a memory that belonged to someone else. He was just a story she heard as a child. He was a hope; he was a wish. That day they spent together was just a story she made up somewhere in the minutes between awake and asleep. Perhaps it was no more than a hallucinatory dream burned into her out of wanting something so much. As if her need to connect with someone had caused a scar inside her that was shaped like an entire day.

If his eyes found their way to her, which they often did, she did not notice it. She only saw him sitting quietly with Mister Hughes at dinner. Smiling in a lackluster way and nodding politely at the man's conversation. Francis would move the food around his plate and would scarcely take a bite. When he did finally consume something, he often looked around the room first, suspiciously, before spooning something nearly inedible into his mouth. Upon swallowing, he would look guilty. You could barely see it, with his hands being under the table, but he would do the sign of the cross. This was done is equal parts out of habit and out of a guilty longing for forgiveness for a sin never committed.

At night after her door was closed, she would hold the book he gave her in her hands, and trace the pencil marks inside the book, the faint traces around words. The small note he gave her had somehow disappeared, and she would often wonder if it had ever been there at all.

The only excitement came as July edged into the beginning of August, it was hardly possible to tell anymore, what the day was, what the week was, and if any of what happened in slow motion all around them was even real.

Isabelle began to realize that everyone at home was right about her. She was tired.

She had always been tired.

More tired than even *she* thought she was.

She was once again living a life ten seconds removed from everyone around her. Whether or not this was the cause of medication or madness, she could not tell.

So, when Agnes sat down across from her at dinner one night, it took some time for Isabelle to lift her head and see this young and dangerous creature before her. Isabelle lifted her head and was paralyzed. Isabelle's eyes did not see the snakes twitching around her face framing it like a painting in a museum. When Isabelle looked at her, she saw a mixture of creeping driftwood, fingers, and guns, all of which seemed to writhe together in a painting that had come horribly to life.

"You're a god-awful bitch," the teenager sneered at Isabelle. "You think you are better than me because you never even tried to kill the man that hurt you, you're wrong. You're worse. You rather have a nice house and all the torture." Agnes seemed to Isabelle like a wild dog, one that would roam the neighborhood until it had to be shot. "My father, he was a good man, he didn't deserve what I did to him, until he did. He deserved it then. I could have killed him; I chose not to, no one cares about that. No one ever thanks me for my kindness. He did deserve it by the end. They all deserve it. They deserve it!" Agnes started yelling. Isabelle could see Mister Hughes and some of the other young men that normally handled the luggage all coming over to her.

"I know what they did to you. They did it to me." As she said this, her arms were already being restrained behind her back. She tried to fight, but all Agnes had left were her words. "Your baby isn't dead Isabelle! Listen to me, he's not dead, neither is my little girl. I know you hear them. You can hear them right now. He's crying for you Isabelle. They're here with us, they're in the walls." The two younger gentlemen were restraining Agnes, an injection was given to her in her upper thigh as she kicked and fought her way through the now very crowded dining room.

Isabelle remained ten seconds delayed; the rest of the dinner crowd seemed to notice this was happening almost at the same time it was ending.

Agnes' exclamations continued, though they began to slow and slur when whatever it was they gave her began finally to take hold of the girl.

"I'm sure you hear him, crying. They have him here somewhere. He's with my little girl. They're together. You're just too stupid to look for them . . ." Agnes was silent then, the life and breathe seemed to be pushed out of her. Her eyes remained open and her jaw hung open and slack.

By the time Isabelle whispered to herself, "He's not dead . . .," Isabelle's other dinner companions were finally beginning to register that Agnes had gotten up from her table.

Isabelle stared through the thick beveled glass window that had been her nightly dinner companion. Until this moment, she had never taken notice of the overly decorative window that did not face out to the sea, but to another hallway. A window that only looked deeper inside this building and not out.

No one noticed. When she smashed her hand through the glass, no one seemed to, except for him.

The glass was thick and rounded, like scar tissue forming over years of wounds, both physical and mental. She had to strike it a few times before she was able to break through. Her hands wrapped around a strong but sturdy piece of the window. It was equal parts beveled glass and soldered metal. It seemed to bend under her hand, not like a knife, but as if it had already become part of her.

The window shard, held tightly in her hand pierced her skin and flesh right above where her heart was.

188

Luckily, she was poor in her aim. The glass broke her skin after it fought its way through the thick layers of her clothing. It was pulled out of her before it was ever allowed to burrow itself all the way in, like an animal tunneling underground for warmth.

She was placed gently on the floor as if she were a baby bird that had fallen from the nest. Cloth napkins were pressed firmly against the wound by strong hands. She could hear a voice that seemed far away keep repeating the words, "Never mind any of this, calm down everyone," and then another voice saying, "It's not as bad as it looks don't you worry, it's really barely a scratch."

She finally noticed . . . ten seconds too late, whose hand it was that was pressed so close to her heart. He stared into her eyes. She saw the scar above his lip, the way it trembled without his mouth moving.

He whispered to her, before she faded into sleep, *"If all else remained, and she were annihilated, the universe would turn to a mighty stranger."*

She heard his words, so close to the exact quote from the book. She did not see his mouth moving, so perhaps it was that Francis had never said anything at all, that she had only wished it so.

Chapter 24

For the next few days after the incident in the dining room, she realized once again that people had taken to whispering when they tried to talk to her. As if they were afraid that sound would disturb her, as if she was a dusty and forgotten book on a top shelf, always out of reach. It would remain there for years, neglected. No one bothering to reach for it and see what was inside.

They kept her in bed for a few days. They said it was not because of her injury, but more because of the shock she had caused herself, and confusion that was created in the aftermath for everyone else.

When Daisy came in to give her a small tray of food, fresh water, and a small vase containing wildflowers, she reassured Isabelle that most of the guests believed that it had been Agnes who hurt her. That even though they had all watched the two women as if they were a show on a grand stage, they did not really know what had happened. "And as far as I'm concerned Ma'am, they can continue thinking that too. We all know you would not have done what you did had she not upset you so much. So, don't worry any about what people here think of you."

"I haven't worried about that. Actually, the thought never crossed my mind," Isabelle said as her hand trembled as she reached for the glass of water. The water itself seemed cloudier than it should have been. It also tasted old; like stale air in the attic crawlspace above her.

Daisy continued to tidy up the room a little, but as Isabelle had barely left her bed in the past days there really was not very much to clean up. She was wiping down the bureaus and mirrors when she whispered, "Why did you do it Ma'am? I know you were upset, but you just don't seem like the type to act up like that." Daisy's voice barely rode against her breath to form words. She sounded almost like phantom echoes from someone in this same room, years before.

"I'm not sure really. It was just something that I did. I didn't even really think about it," Isabelle said. She could not be sure if she were telling the truth. In fact, she barely remembered the incident at all. She did remember thinking of Oscar and wondering about him. She remembered feeling guilty, but she could not be sure why.

"You did give us all a scare; especially Father Francis. I've never seen someone look so worried. He stayed outside your room, sitting on the floor in the hallway. He stayed there all night the first night, maybe even the second one. We shouldn't have let him do it, but what could we say?" Daisy paused, turning slowly back to face Isabelle. Her voice was direct, but her eyes seemed to question as she said, "After all, he's a holy man. He was probably praying for you. Isn't that right Ma'am?"

Isabelle turned her eyes down and stared at her hands and remembered how it felt when he held her hand in his. "Yes, that's right. He was probably praying."

"Oh, I have been forgetting to give this to you." She handed Isabelle another book. "He said you left it at the table that night and he picked it up for you." Daisy's eyes had an almost impish glow when she said this. She looked like a young girl playing a part on the stage.

"That was sweet of you to remember, Daisy, please give Father Francis my thanks as well. I had almost forgotten that I was about to start reading it." Isabelle smiled, turning the book over in her hands and seeing the title of the book in a much-worn gold embossed stamp. She ran her finger over it and could almost feel the faint gold flakes come off against her skin.

"What book is it Ma'am?" Daisy asked her.

"It's Jane Eyre," Isabelle answered, though she knew full well that Daisy would not have ever heard of the book.

"Is it a torrid romance book?" Daisy giggled.

"It is a romance book, I'm not sure if I would call it torrid," Isabelle smiled.

"Well one of these days when you're in the kitchen soaking your hands, you'll have to read the steamiest parts to Nora, and I. Can you imagine? How embarrassed she would be." Daisy continued to laugh as she got her small basket of cleaning supplies together. "Rest well tonight Ma'am, Mister Hughes said he would like you to come down for breakfast in the morning."

"Of course, Daisy, that's no problem. Good night."

"Good night Ma'am"

The door was not even entirely shut before Isabelle opened the book, searching again for a sign, a note, or a message. She realized that one of the pages was folded in on itself. When she unfolded the paper, which was already beginning to darken and curl around the edges, she saw right away that there was a small paragraph circled in pencil.

"Every atom in your flesh is as dear to me as my own: in pain and sickness it would still be dear. Your mind is my treasure, if it were broken, it would be my treasure still."

Isabelle read the words over again, until she was hearing it in his voice. She lifted the book to her chest. She pressed it into the same spot he had held the napkins to stop her bleeding just days ago. As she did this, she saw a small envelope fall from the book. She picked it up immediately and felt that it was still damp from the sea. She tore it open and began reading. It was not until she was about halfway through that she began to understand what it was that she held in her hands.

~

Isabelle-

We have been made aware of the dreadful situation that you have found yourself in. You must understand that is not what we had imagined for you. We hoped that with time away that there could be hope that you would return to us as a changed woman. I have discussed this with Henry, and we have decided that it would be best for you to return to Portland and remain in my care for the time being. We are not sure what more we can do for you, but we will do what is in our power to help you. With the help of God and a Doctor, we are sure that we can help you once again to learn to behave in a proper manner, as a wife, or as a companion to me.

We will arrange with the hotel for your departure at the earliest convenience.

Yours,

Mother Minnie

So, that was it then. As quickly as she was sent here, she was being sent home. Home seemed to her to be a ridiculous word for where she would be going. She thought of Agnes in the attic and realized that the dark world of her imagination was probably far more appealing than her life. The one that poor Agnes was made to endure during the long winter months when she was not here. Protected on all sides by these hotel walls and then again on all sides by the sea. Where was Agnes when she was not here? Isabelle could not see her living anywhere else.

Isabelle walked to the window and stared out at the ocean. It stretched out around her in all directions, the thought of which taunted her and made her apprehensive. The vastness of it, yet still, even in its vastness it would lead back where she came from. The water stretched out in front of her, but the strong current of reality, the tangled grasp of the undertow would always win.

It could happen as soon as tomorrow. She understood that. She could be back on that ship with the half-rotted plants and the empty mailbags.

She watched the time as it passed slowly. The minutes stretched like long feverish nightmares that you find difficult to pull yourself out of even hours after you wake. She sipped the now lukewarm tea. She tasted it for the first time; it was earthy. Like the dankest parts in a wet wood, near a swamp. She knew she should not continue drinking, but every time she put the cup down Oscar's cries would go from his normal wail, to one that was both frightening, and awful.

She sipped again and realized that it was not just Oscar's screams that she was hearing, but her own as well. She never thought of them before now. The feral sounds she made while she was giving birth. Of course, she knew what was supposed to happen; she knew that from the beginning. But she hadn't fully grasped how it would feel. She did not understand it then and she does not understand it now.

How does anyone survive it? She laughed to herself, because of course, some do not . . .

With that thought, Oscar was quiet. Even he must have to rest. His little lungs were barely formed. He had to sleep. One could not expect him to continue these constant screams for all her life. No matter how lonely she realized she was without them.

She was a good mother. She would let him nap; she could tell he had begun to grow weary. She finished her tea; the bottom of the cup had a muddy texture, not like tealeaves at all. More like dirt.

Wet dirt.

Francis always loved the smell of that, he told her.

She looked at the small wind up clock next to her bed and saw that it was just after midnight. Isabelle rose from the bed and walked to her door. She knew that once she opened it her life would go in one of two directions. Either she would join Agnes in the attic, alongside the cobwebs and nightmares, or she would be . . .

She paused before opening it. She pressed her ear to the door, hoping to hear something. Maybe she was hoping to hear a prayer, a hope, a wish.

It was silent.

Isabelle opened the door, and he was there, standing in front of her. He was waiting. All these nights, perhaps even long before the incident in the dining room, he had been there, waiting for her to let him in.

Her breath made a slight sound, and sort of relieved puff. She was not alone. He smiled at her, and then his face folded in on itself. He seemed to collapse while still standing. He began to sob. She stepped forward into him, threw her arms around his neck, and held him tight against her.

For a fleeting moment, she thought they were outside, in a rainstorm. She could feel his hot tears as they dripped down her shoulder and danced down the crease of her spine that was just ever so delicately crooked. It was not noticeable to the eye, but she could feel that tear fall down her back in jagged path, like lightening. She whispered in his ear, "Come in."

She closed the door behind them, and though both knew that no one could hear them, they kept their voices low, barely above a whisper.

"Did you like the book Isabelle?" He asked, wiping the tears from his face, and pretending that they never happened. The way men were always taught to do.

"The letter that was tucked in there . . . Where did you get that letter?" She asked instead.

"That's not an answer to my question Isabelle. Did you like the book?"

"Of course, I did, you knew I would." She said this quickly and with determination that she would not let him lead her through his mind's maze.

"You've read it before then, I thought you probably had. You remind me of her, you know."

"Oh really, which one? Bertha, in the attic?" She laughed because that was who she thought she could so easily become.

"No, of course not, you're Jane of course."

"How did you get the letter Francis?"

"I saw it yesterday; it was on your tray they were bringing you for dinner. I didn't read it, you know that; the envelope was still sealed."

"It came yesterday?" She said this, and her voice rose in volume with the natural terror of it. She knew now that if she was supposed to have read this yesterday that it meant she was probably set to be sent home tomorrow. Which is why Mister Hughes wanted her down for breakfast.

"Was it a love letter Isabelle, from your husband?" He sounded jealous.

"No, it was from his mother. She heard about what happened and they are making me go home. I am not sure when. Maybe tomorrow, I don't know."

"Do you think they are sending you to an asylum?" He asked this but in a leading manner, as if he wanted her to admit to herself and to him that she knew where she was going.

"No, no I think, I don't know, no . . . at least not right away. I think I will be sent to Mother Minnie's, until they can find someplace that will not be too embarrassing for them . . . or until they find a way for him to divorce me and have his social standing not be completely ruined. One of those."

"You broke a window and stabbed yourself; do you really think that they are just going to let you be an old woman's sewing companion?" He paused then and waited for Isabelle to understand what he was saying. He needed her feel the weight of her future.

"I . . . yes, I know," she whispered.

"You don't have to go. You could stay here," he paused and looked at Isabelle who was shaking her head no. "Not in the hotel, but on the Island. We could leave here, together. Tonight. It doesn't have to be what you think it will be. Your life can be your own."

He barely got the words our before she interrupted him. "How? How can that happen, with your money, with my money? We do not own our lives Francis. They belong to someone else. You are owned by the church, my husband owns me . . . I pray every day to your God, the one you do not believe in. I hope he makes me lose my mind. I hope I can turn into Agnes, rocking an empty cradle, living in a dream. Even a nightmare would be better than this slow death of the ordinary. But it is all I have and being fine with that is what I need to be."

"Don't say that." His hand reached to her face, and Isabelle found herself leaning into the palm of his hand. Her head felt heavy, weighed down with a lifetime of believing she was a burden. "Fine, if we can't stay here, I'll go with you." He whispered this, and to Isabelle's ears, it sounded not like a lie, but like a wish, a hope.

"What are you saying Francis? You are not making any sense. Why would you do this? No . . . just, no, I can't . . . you can't." She pulled herself away from his hand. She knew that there was something that existed between them. It was a *thing* that she could not explain away, no matter how much she tried. She also knew that none of that mattered; it couldn't possibly matter at the end of the day, after daylight turned to madness.

Isabelle understood, even if Francis could not, that they only existed like this for each other because of this hotel, because of this summer, on this island. If they had passed each other on a street on just a normal day their eyes would have met, maybe for a moment and that would have been the end of it. It would have been a story untold. She knew that meeting him here in this broken off sliver of her life was just another way that fate was reminding her that she was alone. She had been, since she was young.

Could she love him if she would let herself? Of course, she could. She could fall into him as if he were the ocean she had always feared but could not allow herself to live far from. If she were to allow him to love her . . . that would be more difficult. She never felt comfortable with that, which was why at the end of the day, perhaps Henry made the most sense. He did not love her, and to her . . . maybe that was better. It was easier on the heart at the end of the day if all it had to do was keep beating. It would never need to exhaust itself on love. The imaginary bronze burnished walls that surrounded her heart would shine in the sunlight protecting her.

It was safer.

She was not strong enough for love; it could break whatever was left of her. She would prefer to have the memory rather than a painful reality that would bruise and fade over time. Molly's kiss and Francis' hand on hers. If they could plait themselves together with Oscar's screams, she could live inside that beautiful nightmare forever.

"You need to leave; I have to rest. I am sure tomorrow will be exhausting. I still need to pack my things." She paused, trying to fish
199

the words out of the tidal pool inside her head. All she could seem to find was the feeling of that Starfish, as it lived for a few brief moments in her hands. "If you would like me to return your books, I can give them to you."

"They were a gift," he said as he stepped back from her, as if she were a fireplace that burned too hot. "Keep them; you should have something of your own when you go back there." Francis turned away from her then, and though she could not be certain she thought she saw his lip tremble again. "You're breaking my heart, and yours. I hope you know that." He turned and looked at her, and she thought that perhaps it was for the last time.

"Yes, I know. I'm sorry," she said.

He walked back over towards her, leaned in, and kissed just to the side of her right eye, hitting her temple and a little of her hair. There was an angry tenderness in it, and she knew he was right about their hearts breaking. He turned away then and straightened himself up. His chest almost puffed up with pride that she was sure was a false costume he was putting on for her benefit, or perhaps it was just so he could fool himself.

He walked out of the room but did not close the door. A part of both of them thought she would run after him, fall into him, fall into their imagined life.

She did not.

She closed the door, leaving the silent loneliness of the hallway to continue on without her. It was then that she realized that Oscar has been quiet this whole time. He was such a good boy; he knew Mommy needed the quiet to talk.

She proceeded to pack her things, knowing in her heart that even though no one had said anything to her, that tomorrow would be her last morning here. When she was done locking away her things for safekeeping, she sat at the foot of her bed. She could hear Agnes above her, the rocking of her silent child. Her little girl lost.

That was when she whispered it, "Oscar? Where are you?" She was met with only silence, save for the creaking of the attic rocking chair. "Oscar?"

Isabelle cupped her hand over her ears, opened, and closed her mouth as if she was popping her eardrums, the way she would when she was small and had the type of ear infection that would make pressure build inside her head for days and only eventually abate when blood would leak onto the pillowcase at night.

Still, she was only kissed with silence. She could not even hear the ocean from where she was now; sitting in a silent tower, overlooking the sea. She relaxed herself onto the bed dressed, as she would be tomorrow for breakfast. She thought sleep would come take her away, and she was scared. A night of silent rest was something she realized she might not be ready for.

She pressed her hand into the wound above her heart, the tender wound was already starting to scab over. She looked at it every day in a strange anticipation of seeing black vines growing out of it and reaching towards her heart.

But they never grew.

On this, her last night, she kept the enemy of sleep away, but just barely. She hoped that Oscar would come back to her in the night, or perhaps she hoped it would be Francis. She could see a string of candles tying them together. That string attached underneath their hearts, as Mister Rochester talked of in Jane Eyre.

As the sun began to pull itself up and out of the ocean and into the sky, each candle was blown out, until all there was left was a rope that tied her to nothing.

Chapter 25

"You are looking wonderful this morning Isabelle. You look so rested, and so healthy." Mister Hughes said these words, but Isabelle, who existed ten seconds removed from him, could see that instead of looking into her eyes when he said these words, his head was turned almost all the way around. His eye's followed Daisy alone, as she moved in and out from between the breakfast tables, as if she were not a Daisy, but a hummingbird, or a flower petal dancing on a breeze. It was then that she remembered Mister Hughes calling her Petal, on that first day. She let her gaze travel over the rest of the room, she saw Agnes' face, brimming with jealousy as she looked at Daisy. Isabelle saw Patricia, already sitting alone at a breakfast table. Her lips trembling as she stared out with blank eyes.

The bile rose in Isabelle's mouth, she swallowed it down, afraid that it would turn into a scream if she let it out.

Oscar was still silent.

It was almost as if he had never cried at all . . .

"I am feeling good this morning Sir." Isabelle said, raising her voice a touch louder in hopes of getting his eyes off his normal morning task, which seemed now just to consist of visually raping a young maid.

"I didn't want to tell you before we had all the arrangements for you . . . but you are going home. Today! Isn't that fantastic news! You have done such a good job here and you are doing so much better . . ." His eyes trailed back to Daisy's large skirt as it swished back and forth, as she moved between the tables.

Isabelle steeled her voice as she said, "I did receive a letter that was hinting at that, but I dared not believe it." She plastered a grotesque and garish smile across her face. As if she was a sick adornment spouting water from a church that lacks attendance due to its seeming frightening on the outside.

"Oh yes, it's true. You are going home to your mother and your husband," he said, as he turned his head back to her. His smiled lagged a little and seemed to arrive too late to this morning party.

"Oh . . . She's not my mother. She is my husband's mother," Isabelle said with a pointedness that she hoped would cut like an icicle falling from a window.

"Even better," Mister Hughes said, as if he was reading from a script that was memorized so long ago that the words have since lost their meaning. It was as if he was just making sounds instead of speaking. The way she and Molly would do when they were young and sitting in the dark in their beds, waiting and hoping that sleep would take them away. They would whisper to each other, "Word is a weird word, word is a weird word, word is a weird word," repeatedly. The Girls would take turns until they would burst into giggles. There unabashed laughter came out of them like a butterfly out of a cocoon, it took wings and soared out of that darkened room.

Mister Hughes rapped against her table twice as if he were knocking a secret code to a clubhouse made in a childhood wood. "Enjoy your breakfast, take a last look around. If you need help getting your things together, I am sure Petal can help you." He looked at her again, almost as if he had forgotten to whom he was talking. "The ship boards at 11:45 and leaves here at half past twelve." He smiled in an overly wide gesture. He reached out and was about to place his hand
204

on her shoulder before he drew back, thinking better of it "You will be back in your old life by the time you are cooking dinner tonight."

Of course, he did not hear the screaming damnation in his own voice. He did not know that underneath his words was a condemnation of a person who was being hanged for a crime that had never happened.

"So . . .," he continued, "we will see you on the docks sometime before noon. If your bags are packed . . ."

"Yes, Mister Hughes, they were packed last night," she said.

"Well then, I will have one of the boys up to pick them up later this morning," he paused, and looked at her, almost as if it were the first time. He placed his hand heavily on her shoulder at that point. It seemed to weigh her down, like stones in her pockets. "You are a good girl Isabelle. You did the best you could."

If his eyes were dead or predatory, she could not tell anymore.

Her eyes scanned the room for the rest of the breakfast hour; they never found their home in Francis' face. He was nowhere, but he was everywhere inside of her.

She whispered into her uneaten plate of eggs benedict, for Oscar to come to her. She wanted in some way to be blanketed in his cries, made full in her stomach from his three minutes of longing.

It never happened.

She ate her last meal here on this island, alone. She was the queen of these nightmares of hers, which were quickly being forgotten and swept out to sea. Francis never came down that morning. It was for the better, she told herself.

There was no need for sadness to become fetishized in these final moments here. They had agreed to break each other's hearts. To break each other into pieces, but not to ruin each other to the point of not being able to ever be put whole again. He deserved more than that.

Of course, when they were being sewn back together, there was a good chance that pieces would be missing in the end, but that did not matter. She was broken before, and seemingly sewn back together almost right, but not quite.

By the time she entered her room after breakfast, all her belongings had been removed and taken to the dock. The only thing remaining was a bundle of wilted lilacs that grew all summer in the shady part of the hotel's back property, and of course, the copy of Jane Eyre that she had tucked under the mattress, hidden away the same way she had painted Oscar's initial in her own blood.

She tucked the book deep inside her now loosely laced corset. It rested against her body; much the way armor rested against a body of a boy too young ever to see war. She could feel the book's edges against her lower ribs. If she breathed in and out the way she wanted, she would have felt the constriction of its words against her.

It was a secret code that she understood but could never speak aloud.

Isabelle made it halfway down the dock towards the ship. There was an anticipation that fluttered inside of her that made her think of equal parts doomsday stories and Christmas at the same time. She stopped short, about twenty feet from boarding. She watched her small assortment of baggage being placed on the ship with little to no care. Her belongings were thrown on there with the same kind of disregard that the rotted plants were. As she was about to board the ship she asked, "Is there more time before the ship departs. I believe I forgot a book in my room." Isabelle made her eyes wide as she asked it.

A man who was made more of beard than human replied, "We leave in about thirty minutes Ma'am. Seeing it's such a nice day you might want to get back early so you can get a seat outside."

"Thank you, yes. I will not be long, just a few minutes. I shouldn't have been so careless." Isabelle turned her back on the ship, and on her belongings. On her life that existed before the island.

Before this summer hotel.

She walked briskly. She felt herself becoming almost winded as she approached the end of the dock. She remembered the way Francis breathed heavily on their walk.

She got to the mouth of the hotel and looked around. Hoping to see him, hoping to hear Oscar's cries, telling her that she was close, close to what she was searching for . . . She was met with silence, and isolation. Francis was not here waiting for her on the steps, leaning against that post where she so often had sat vigil.

She looked back towards the ship one more time to see if there was anyone there who was truly bearing witness to where she was going. There was no one looking, no one watching out for her.

She walked quickly towards the shadows that clung like scared children to the hotel. She found herself running past the gazebo and the little path that wound its way to the cemetery with the small sad mounds of earth, those pathetic piles of wet dirt that Francis loved the smell of so much.

She walked past there, her legs growing stronger with each step. The book that was tied into her chest no longer seemed to constrict her air, but instead to shield her from the mistake that she could have become.

When she got to the tidal pools that were filled with angry sea birds and the mid-day sun, she thought she would have seen him . . . but he was not there.

Isabelle closed her eyes and tried to remember his hand on hers, but there was nothing. There was only the salt-slicked grime of the sea breeze as it crept in from the deep. With her eyes still closed, she thought of Oscar, his ever-present cries through the summer, which somehow seemed more real than his three minutes of wailing when he was born.

Still there was nothing.

Her feet began to slip a little as she walked on the rocks, edging closer to the thing she always feared. The water.

The alone.

She stood there, letting the sea grab at her legs, only to let her go at the last minute. She waited so patiently she thought, to hear Oscar cry again, but he was not there with her. Whatever there was of him was still safely packed away in that beautiful hatbox, only water damaged on the outside. She thought Francis would also be there with her, but in the end, she was right all along. He only existed in the part of her that was broken off, polished, and made to shine again for a few brief weeks she had here. The queen of all her sins.

Everything else was this.

Only this.

Her feet began to slip against the rocks. One landed in a tidal pool that lived for today at a steep angle facing the sea.

She regretted that she had been afraid of the sea birds as their wings beat against her skirt. She regretted that she had not opened her eyes when Molly kissed her. She regretted that she was told she was nothing, and that she was alone and that she had believed it.

She regretted all of that, as her other foot slipped off the rock.

She thought it better if she were not to fight it.

The thing she regretted most of all was that it was Henry's words that rang in her ears as she allowed her second foot to *slip* off the rock completely.

She regretted that she had not taken a larger breath before the water slammed into her chest like knives. She could almost feel that

208

grundylow from her youth reach out of the dark and grab her ankle. If she had wanted it more, she could have felt Francis' hand warp around her wrist . . . except it did not. It was not there, not now.

She wondered why, in the moments before her skull slammed into stone and she became nothing, why it was she lived a life that no one would ever know about?

She did not know if she meant for things to end this way, but as the breath left in her lungs turned into a burning fire, she was not regretting that they did.

Not the end . . .

Sneak Peek into

When the Sleeping Dead Still Talk

(The Hotel Book II)

Coming November 2020

Chapter 1

Francis...the morning of

Francis' bones felt stiff and weary. There was a heaviness to his body, as he laid on his bed. His hand reached out for the filthy glass of whiskey that was sleeping near to him. That bitter brown liquid, it was his life; it was his wife . . .

He found it empty. He tried to reach for the bottle but instead he knocked it over. It sounded empty and made the room echo in a surreal loneliness as the bottle rolled under his bed.

His room was on the second floor in the corner of the west wing. Close to the room that contained the showers. The floors in the rooms surrounding his all had slanting floors and a wet musty smell. Like stale water leaking slowly over years, just underneath the wood.

When he was sent here the first time, three years ago, The Monsignor had given him a small bag of glass marbles. He made a joke to Francis that he "should make sure to keep hold of these marbles, as you've lost the rest of yours already." It was a phrase that Francis never heard before and after asking about it, he realized it was an insult hidden inside a gift. Those were the strangest kinds.

As a child, gifts were not something that were given out in his house. Father Bertrand, an older Priest at Saint Anne's who spoke with a thick French-Canadian accent, had over the years become a benevolent father figure to Francis, and ignored Francis' excessive drinking. Francis loved Bertrand and had always felt he had known the man his entire life; that somehow as long as there had been a Francis, there had been a Bertrand.

On the nights where Francis' mind was burning with thoughts, anger, and over activity, he would take out the small bag of glass marbles and would roll them on his crooked floor in his crooked room. He would watch the marbles bounce of the walls and pick up speed, careening into each other before eventually finding their place in the very lowest point in the room. Underneath Francis' bed, directly where he would lay his head at night.

This irony was not lost on him.

So, this morning as the empty bottle of whiskey rolled under his bed, he heard the bottle as it connected with the marbles, his lost marbles. They seemed to dance for a minute under his bed; the glass sounded like nails scrapping against wood, or like summer hail as it fell angry from the sky.

He laughed, he was not sure why, but he did. He could not remember when he had last slept, he thought it was probably sometime in the days before Isabelle had her *accident.*

"Her accident."

There were so many accidents in his life. The most memorable one probably was when his father had "accidentally" broken a glass and then "accidentally" punched a young Francis in the face with it.

He laughed again, an almost hyena sounding howl. He got up from his bed, paced his floor around his bed. He mumbled the Our Father to himself; a habit he had since childhood. Back when he thought his God was listening. Now he knew his God wasn't there at all, but something was listening.

For years, he would do this, mumble his prayers, and think to himself that he knew there was something more in this world for him. He could feel it …there was another part of him, another part of his soul that was missing.

Then she walked into his life; his Isabelle, a dream born into reality. He did not believe in God, not anymore. Now he only believed in her. He knew there had to be a way to make her believe in him the same way.

He got down on his hands and knees to look under his bed. His body was tired, but his mind, his mind . . . was alert. He was awake. More now than he had even been before. He could hear her singing in the air; he could feel her on the other end of the building. The strings inside his chest, tugging below his heart, he felt them move with her. He could feel them being pulled to tension, stretching far apart from each other . . . she would come back though.

She was an ocean wave, a current. She was a constant, like the tides.

Acknowledgements

My first thank you has to go out to all of you who bought and read this book. I hope you fell in love with Isabelle and Francis as much as I did. Francis' (and perhaps Isabelle's) story continues in my next book, so don't fear!

This novel was originally going to be my first novel, but alas, I was bogged down in research and panic, and when I sat down to write this, my other novel Beautiful, Frightening, and Silent came out instead. Everything happens for a reason, and I am thankful to all the people I have been talking about "Isabelle and Francis" to, for the past countless years.

I want to thank my editor Patty McCarthy. Thank you for understanding my voice, and the poetry that's blended in with the madness.

Thank you to Michelle and Bill for Beta Reading. Thank you to Nadine for the help in research.

Thank you to all my friends and students (there are too many to mention) who support me and believe in me.

Thank you to my book besties and my Vox Vomitus Vixens, Allison, and Trisha. I don't know if I could have done any of this without you both.

Thank you to Aaron, and Crystal, and Abby, and Jack, and Chella, Pam, James, and Daniel…and so many more. You are my book family, thank you for helping when I need help, listening when I need to vent, and being part of this journey.

Thank you to Pam Stack (and everyone involved with the Global Authors on the Air Network (again too many of you to name).

Thank you to Julie and the team at Books and Moods PR, thank you to Annie and Lily at Partners in Crime Book Promotion. Thank you to all the book bloggers and Bookstagrammers!

Thanks to my Mom and my Dad (though he is not with us), I hope this makes you both proud.

Huge amount of love to my best friend and life-long "pen pal" Tara, who talked me down off creative cliffs, and for encouraging me when I needed it, and getting angry alongside me when I needed that.

Thank you to my baby dog Lord Tubby who barked at me until I played with him every time that he knew I really needed a break.

Finally, my partner in life, Roman. You are the best part of all my days, thank you for giving me the time, the space, and the encouragement to do all of this. You are my muse. I love you Buster.

If you liked the book, please head over to Good Reads or Amazon and leave a review!! If you hated the book, maybe don't do that.

Cover Design: Don Noble – Rooster Republic Press

About the Author

Jennifer Anne Gordon is a gothic horror novelist. Her debut novel, Beautiful, Frightening, and Silent broke presale records with her publisher, and has received critical acclaim.

She had a collection of her mixed media artwork published during spring of 2020, entitled Victoriana: mixed media art of Jennifer Gordon

Jennifer is one of the hosts and the Creator of Vox Vomitus, a videocast on the Global Authors on the Air Network.

Jennifer is a pale curly haired ginger, obsessed with horror, ghosts, abandoned buildings, and her dog "Lord Tubby".

She graduated from the New Hampshire Institute of Art, where she studied Acting. She also studied at the University of New Hampshire with a concentration in Art History and English.

She has made her living as an actress, a magician's assistant, a "gallerina", a painter, and burlesque performer and for the past 10 years as an award-winning professional ballroom dancer, performer, instructor, and choreographer.

When not scribbling away (ok, typing frantically) she enjoys traveling with her fiancé and dance partner, teaching her dog ridiculous tricks (like 'give me a kiss' and 'what hand is the treat in?') as well as taking photos of abandoned buildings and haunted locations.

For more information and benevolent stalking, please visit her website at www.JenniferAnneGordon.com